"There is a great reckoning in the di\ ▌▌▌▌ *Thunder*, and Pastor B. F. Randall is hei cinating and factual in his ability to co in a dramatic way. He brings us right into jerusalem as history plays out before our eyes. An inspired retelling from the perspective of Jesus' younger brother, James, this book immerses readers in the uncertainty, the panic, and the relief that comes along in finding the truth: Jesus is Lord. Readers are enlightened as James discovers just who his big brother *really* is."

—Laura Lynn Hughes
speaker, advocate, best-selling author of *Choose Zoe*

"Put yourself in the shoes of James, the younger brother of Jesus. Imagine growing up with Jesus—the perfect son, sinless brother, model citizen ... and then He is arrested. Imagine the conflicting feelings James struggles with as he travels to Jerusalem to see for himself what has transpired. In *Between the Lightning and the Thunder*, B. F. Randall beautifully captures James's struggles with the past, the present, and the future. This book is a must-read for everyone who has already fallen in love with James. Join him on his unforgettable journey."

—Carol Fitchhorn
author of *Wisps of Wisdom: A Devotional Journal*

"*Between the Lightning and the Thunder* caused me to reflect on the writings of C. S. Lewis, which were greatly influenced by his faith and desire to present biblical truth through the telling of his stories. They caused you to dig below the surface, to think and ponder the deeper truths revealed in the pages. I also found this to be true with B. F.'s work. I have often thought of this younger brother of the Lord but had never fully contemplated what a challenge and struggle it must have been for him to even consider that this man Jesus, his brother, might possibly be the promised Messiah. B. F. skillfully moves us through the pages to engage on a divine journey with a doubting brother who comes to recognize Jesus not only as his brother but also as his Lord. Fiction you say, I'm not so sure. Perhaps my friend and Pastor B. F. Randall is closer to the truth than we know. Great story, my friend. *Between the Lightning and the Thunder* is a great read."

—Leo C. Price
Leo Calvin Price Ministries, author of *The Sixth Dragon* and
Taking the IF Out of Life

"In this engaging novel, B. F. Randall has tapped into the transformative journey of a little brother, a skeptic, and one who followed at a distance to a leading apostle who would lay down his life for his savior. The connections and parallels to the doubts and struggles of faith that we all face draw us into the narrative and speak straight to the heart. I believe the pages of this book will give you a fresh glimpse of the Messiah and call you to a deeper love and commitment to Jesus."

—Dave Patterson
pastor, The Father's House, Vacaville, CA

"B. F. Randall is a trusted voice, a man of integrity and creativity. He has a passion to help people understand the stories of the Bible. I love how this fictional book describes the transformation of James, the younger brother of Jesus, from his doubts to his understanding of his destiny. Once you begin reading this unfolding story, you will certainly find it difficult to put it down. The story is written brilliantly and is creatively authentic. Check this book out."

—Terry Mahan
The Father's House Church, Leesburg, FL

"Go ahead! Dive in! Take this heart journey with James as he recalls his brother's life and death, constantly revealing just one more reason his brother was, and is, truly the Lord! Yes, Jesus. As each event is unveiled, you'll find that author B. F. Randall has settled into his own unique way of making Jesus real and alive. Get ready for mind-stimulating thoughts and emotions! The book is written exquisitely yet simply, and I was captured by Randall's powerful yet relaxing style as if the thunder and lightning were gently shouting to my own heart! Thank you, B. F.!"

—Paula Stefanovich Price
songwriter, solo artist, and speaker

"B. F. Randall has masterfully written about the experience of Jesus' brother, James. It is a riveting story detailing the human emotions James must have experienced at the foot of the cross and in the days that followed. B. F. writes this story in such color that we feel it is our experience. After all, it is, isn't it? We've all doubted our faith at one time or another. However, *Between the Lightning and the Thunder* is sure to make each of us feel our humanity and recognize that we're not so abnormal after all."

—Kevin Goff
speaker, pastor, The Rock Church, Goodyear, AZ

BETWEEN THE
LIGHTNING
AND THE
THUNDER

B. F. RANDALL

BROOKSTONE
PUBLISHING GROUP
Birmingham, Alabama

Between the Lightning and the Thunder

Brookstone Publishing Group
An imprint of Iron Stream Media
100 Missionary Ridge
Birmingham, AL 35242
IronStreamMedia.com

Library of Congress Control Number: 2022912254

Cover design by Hannah Linder Designs

ISBN: 978-1-949856-73-6 paperback
ISBN: 978-1-949856-74-3 eBook

1 2 3 4 5—27 26 25 24 23

Roberta, my wife, my lover, my best friend.
Always at my side, encouraging, supporting, and assisting.
My spell-checker, grammar corrector, and in-house editor.
I don't know what I'd do without you.
I love you to the moon and beyond.
(She even corrected this ~~dedacation~~ dedication!)

CONTENTS

CONTENTS

CHAPTER ONE
Ambushed by Regret

Thirty years in his shadow. Watching, learning, following his lead. He was my friend, my mentor, my brother. We played together, worked, laughed, and cried together.

But now it was over.

We would never talk again. No more plans. No more dreams. I would never again be able to say I love you. Or I'm sorry.

Sitting against the rough surface of an old, twisted olive tree, I stared into the darkness. My mind reeled. What went wrong? What should I have done? What could I do?

Tears ran down my cheeks as my heart cried out in despair: stop—please—please stop. Desperate to escape the horror of my brother's crucifixion, I gazed into the heavens and asked the question whose answer would bring no relief. Why? Why did he have to die? Why did he have to suffer so?

What had been a brisk cool day with clear blue skies turned dark. Foreboding. The temperature rose sharply. Black, ominous clouds flashed overhead with a language all their own. With a deep sigh, I traced over the day's events— scenes I desperately wanted to avoid but could not.

I shifted my weight to blend into the misshapen trunk of the tree and pulled my legs in tight. Reflection refreshed the pain in my heart and brought new tears to my inflamed eyes.

What now? What was I supposed to do now?

The heavens answered with an explosion of bright streaks of light that formed a distorted hand pointing toward the hill called Golgotha, which meant "the place of the skull." With my attention drawn to the repulsive mound of death, the day replayed in my mind.

∞

The journey from Nazareth to Jerusalem was long and miserable. The roads—if you want to call them roads—had been obliterated by the hooves of horses and donkeys and the wheels of carts and chariots. The countless herds and flocks driven to their demise for our culinary enjoyment helped turn the roads into mere dusty paths overladen with jagged stones, deep potholes, and layer upon layer of animal dung. Every step became an excursion of misery.

With each step I took, the same questions arose: Why had we ventured out on that unpleasant journey? Was there some long past religious obligation we needed to fulfill? Were we drawn by a divine unction to bring our offerings and to worship at God's altar in humble adoration?

No. We were on a mission with a different objective: to retrieve a wayward son and sibling—my brother Jesus. This wasn't a unique undertaking but a repeated effort to again rescue our family's eldest son from the consequences of his foolishness. This time was different, though, because his recklessness was perceived as rebellion.

After a man died, the firstborn son was expected to assume the responsibility for the family and to carry on his father's work. This was true for every family—but ours. My elder brother had much loftier goals. At least that is what he often said.

After our father died, Jesus assumed his obligations with earnest—for a while. Until one day he announced the time had come for him to leave, to commence what became an absurd obsession. I am the second born, so the family's care became my responsibility, and my life became one perpetual trek along rocky roads and dust-covered trails in pursuit of a brother whose antics showed little concern for any of his kin. I lost count of the cities, villages, and hamlets we went through to find him. When we did, we spent endless hours trying to persuade him to return home where he belonged.

On one such occasion, my brothers and I accompanied Mama to a home where a large crowd had gathered. We couldn't push our way through, so one of his followers, who recognized Mama, went in and told him we were outside. I heard him say that we were not his family, that his family were those who followed him. Although I knew he meant no harm, statements like that broke Mama's heart and angered me to my core.

Few doubted that he had lost his mind. Our brother Simon thought Jesus had slipped away from reality long before he left home. Although our other brothers, Joses and Judas, held out hope that he would come to his senses, they, too, saw how unstable he had become. Even Mariam—loving, committed, and tolerant as she was—no longer excused him.

One holdout remained. Mama. She seemed to see something in him that no one else could. But this time was different. He had pushed beyond Mama's ability to overlook his recklessness. It had become a potentially dangerous problem.

I stepped beside Mama, placed my arm around her shoulder, and pulled her close to me. "Stay close. We're almost there."

Extending my other hand behind me, I waved slightly, then felt Mariam's hand slip into mine. "You stay close too, sister."

We maneuvered through the crowd, past squealing children, around traders and hawkers, and through the arch into Jerusalem. The streets teemed with merchants and Passover pilgrims. Excitement hung heavy over the city. Ahead, the towers of the Fortress of Antonia at the northwest corner of the temple rose before us. There we would find my wayward brother who, no doubt, waited for us to retrieve him from the stench of Roman incarceration.

We ambled through a mass of vendors promoting their wares, hagglers wringing out every ounce of a bargain, and a sea of first-time pilgrims mesmerized by the noise and excitement. I felt better about our trip, confident that the next time we came to Jerusalem, we would be a part of the festivities.

Unfortunately, not this time.

My big brother had carried his declarations and assertions too far, and we had come to rescue not celebrate.

He had never been arrested before. His public demonstrations often caught the attention of the Sanhedrin and the Temple Guard but never to the point of being arrested. I was sure the time he spent in the bowels of the Roman prison or

Herod's dungeon would have shaken some common sense into him.

At the Praetorium, I looked for a place for Mama and Mariam to rest. Two large men, talking and eating fruit, perched on the only stone bench within eyesight of the entrance to Pilate's Stone Pavement. They looked up at me apathetically when we approached, until their gaze turned to Mama. When their eyes met hers, their expressions changed, as if they were looking into their own mothers' eyes. Both men grabbed their knapsacks, stood, and smiled. "Please sit here," one of them said, and both stepped away.

I placed my bag on the ground and gently guided Mama to the bench. She sat and leaned against the wall with a slight groan of relief. I doubled my cloak, placed it behind her back, and tenderly positioned her against the wall. Shaded from the sun, she and Mariam could rest while I rescued Jesus. I took a couple of steps toward the crowd and searched for any sign of him.

"Can you see him?" Mama said in a tone filled with concern. Her gentle voice was the only true motive I had for continuing these efforts to salvage my brother from his foolishness.

"No, Mama," I called over my shoulder. "They haven't brought him out yet."

Most Passover pilgrims, it seemed, came here to get a look at where judgment would be dispensed: the Pavement. They wanted to witness the Procurator of Emperor Tiberius perform his parody of justice.

Bounded by a prominent stone barrier, a huge throne sat center stage with its massive golden eagle overhead— all devised to impress spectators and to demonstrate the authority of Rome. It accomplished its purpose to validate Caesar's contempt for the inhabitants of Judea.

The stone barrier erected to separate Jerusalem from the sovereign soil of Rome was shorter than the average man, and it extended from Pilate's palace to the Jaffa Gate. The entrance onto the enormous limestone pavement was wide and unobstructed. No sentry stood guard at the entrance because no self-respecting Jew would defile himself by stepping foot onto gentile land when the Passover was at hand. Such defilement would make him unclean and unable to enter the temple courts. The Romans did not need to keep us out; our sanctimonious dogma did that.

"Pilate has not arrived. It will be a while yet," I shouted to Mama.

Pilate, no doubt, was waiting for just the right moment to make his grand entrance. For a Roman, the only thing better than power was recognition and reverence. He would strut in like a pompous peacock and take his place of dominance over the masses of Hebrew grubs. There he would play god over the lives of a people who would say and do nothing but wait for some divine intervention to save them. Since the time of Abraham, we had faced oppression and conflict, and each time we withdrew like a turtle in its shell to await God's involvement.

All my life I had heard the ancient stories. I listened to Papa speak of the great victories over our enemies, God's miraculous intervention, and the leaders of renowned wisdom and bravery. I did not know when it happened, but the miraculous and the brave had disappeared. Enraged bullies who called themselves patriots were all that was left in a nation of meek, frightened people.

I should not leave out God's ultimate answer to our national predicament. The messiah. The most repeated story echoed in the ears of the hopeless was that of a messiah. He would be a king whose power would eradicate our Roman tormentors and set us free.

Well, I hoped he'd come soon. For now, my mind wasn't on the hope of a messiah saving us from Rome's tyranny. My concern rested on my family and a brother who had lost all sense of reason. A brother who dashed any of my youthful dreams by failing to shoulder his responsibility.

My mind swam with what could have been until a high-pitched trumpet blast disrupted my daydream. A well-fed centurion, bulging from around his armored breastplate like a melon stuffed into a wineskin, bellowed, "Silence! Let there be order and silence! The envoy of Rome, the voice of Tiberius Caesar, prefect of all Judea, your governor, Pontius Pilate!"

He stepped aside and a pale, bald man stepped out from the shade of the porch canopy. He wore the robes and sash of Roman authority, but in the company of the virile centurions, this frail little man seemed out of place.

This was the governor of all Judea—the ruthless, cunning Pontius Pilate whom I had heard much about?

He mounted the block steps, then deposited his slumped frame onto the great judgment seat. I was filled with a unique sense of relief and a twinge of superiority. Seated in the massive stone chair adorned with images of lions, serpents, and eagles, he looked more like a child to be pitied than a nemesis to be feared.

I looked back at Mama and reassured her with a smile and a wave. Soon she would be on her way back to Nazareth with her strong-willed and, no doubt, humbled son.

Because of Passover, most of those held for minor offenses were often released by midday. They were only required to humble themselves and cower when they passed Pilate's judgment seat. He'd give them a disdainful look, then dismiss their offenses to show his kindness and Rome's leniency. Send them on their way with a warning and a few pokes from the butt of a centurion's lance.

Pilate waved a flaccid hand in the direction of one of the centurion guards and leaned on an ornately carved armrest. The guard grasped a large, iron loop on the door below the portico and pulled with a grunt to expose a cavernous black hole that led down to prison cells below.

"Out!," he shouted into the darkness.

Silence fell over the horde of observers.

"All of you! Out!"

After a long, soundless moment, a dirty, disheveled, bearded figure stepped from the cavern. He raised his hand to block the sun but still strained to see his next step through the glare. Behind him followed several more unkempt men, all clothed in grimy, torn rags. They, too, hadn't been exposed to the light of the sun in some time. Before the guard slammed the heavy wooden door shut, I counted five in all, neither chained nor bound. Jesus was not among them.

With a sneer, Pilate waved a limp wrist toward the portly centurion.

From the sash around his waist, the centurion removed a parchment and read the charges. "Disruption of the peace and tranquility of the jurisdiction of Rome," he shouted, while two other centurions pushed the men in front of Pilate's throne.

With heads bowed, eyes to the ground, the five stood stooped over and shook like dogs about to be beaten.

"Five lashes each, then release them," Pilate said without so much as a glance in their direction. After he rendered the verdict, they were escorted through the archway and into the darkness to await their punishment and discharge.

In more serious matters, a fine might be levied or compulsory labor required. For the most grievous violations, flogging or even death could be imposed. Of course, that was of no concern. The most heinous crime Jesus could have committed would have been the disruption of the peace with his opinionated discourses. Confident the day's most serious offenders were judged and sentenced, I worked my way back through the crowd to Mama.

"He will be out soon, then we can be on our way," I said with my hand on her frail shoulder. Her eyes did not display any hope of a quick departure; instead, they seemed to reflect a knowledge of something far more sinister. "I'm sure we'll be together soon," I said. "A night in there can only make him more aware of his foolishness."

From the thoroughfare that led from the temple, the shouts of a boisterous mob could be heard drawing near. I rose and looked toward the commotion. The elaborate headdresses and garments of the priests and members of the Sanhedrin were unmistakable. Their small but decorative parade made its way along the access between the buildings. People parted like the sea before Moses whenever an assemblage of religious leaders passed. Caiaphas, the high priest, stopped at a low point in the wall, turned, and raised his hand, silencing the rowdy horde that followed him. Caiaphas caught Pilate's eye.

The governor stood and looked at the heavy centurion. "Bring out the Nazarene."

The guard nodded. He pulled open the second wooden door and revealed another cavernous, dismal hole. This time the guard did not bark orders. Instead, he stepped down into the darkness and reappeared moments later with a figure that scarcely resembled a human. Hunched forward, bound hand and foot, the figure labored to take each step.

The man's vestments, face, and hair were matted with mud. A purple robe was thrown loosely over his shoulders, and what resembled a Civic Crown of twisted thorns pierced his head. Some in the crowd snickered. Others laughed while he shuffled onto the Pavement. Weak and unsteady, he appeared close to collapse. He stopped and stood in front of Pilate's throne with his back to me.

Pilate raised a hand. The crowd went silent.

In a loud voice, the governor said, "Are you a king?"

The man spoke softly as he swayed like a stalk of wheat in the wind. Pilate leaned in to hear the answer. He sat back and stared for a long moment, then said, loud enough for all to hear, "What is truth?"

This brought an uproarious response from the mob; however, when Pilate stood, silence again filled the court.

"Look," he said to the crowd, "I have brought him out to you to let you know I find no basis for a charge against him."

With a nod to the guard, the man was turned to face us. The purple robe fell from his shoulders, revealing that his undergarment had been pulled down below his waist. Nearly every part of his body was covered in blood and open wounds. He lifted his head slightly and looked at his accusers through blackened eyes nearly swollen shut.

A hush fell over the crowd. Some grimaced. Some turned away. Others stood stunned by the evidence of Roman cruelty before them.

"Here is the man," shouted Pilate.

My legs felt like they were about to give way beneath me. I stumbled back. I recognized the fabric of the man's garment, woven on my sister's loom and sewn together by my mother's hands.

Here before us like an abused animal, though barely recognizable, was Jesus. My brother.

This was no criminal, no rebellious decadent, but a simple carpenter. A man who has never committed a crime in his life.

My heart ached. I looked back. Mama and Mariam were still seated. The crowd blocked their view. I prayed that God would continue to blind their eyes and silence their ears. I began to feel sick to my stomach, and in a futile attempt to bring some rationale to this horrid situation, I prayed that one day we would see this as a lesson learned. A hideous, repulsive one to be sure.

I pressed forward to hear what admonishment Pilate would give.

The governor turned toward the mob and focused his attention on Caiaphas and the priests. "You brought me this man as an instigator of rebellion among the people. I sent him to Herod, who returned him without charge. You were present when I questioned him. I found your accusations baseless." After a dramatic pause, he continued, "I have punished him, but I have no more reason to hold him."

Caiaphas turned to the crowd and shouted, "He wants to release this blasphemer. This must not be allowed. This must not be allowed!"

The mob erupted with such emotion that my first thought was for Mama's safety. Obscenities and accusations filled the air, but one word stood out above the clamor. A word that shook me to my core: "Crucify!"

Crucify?

My brother was not a blasphemer or a king but a humble, misguided man from a small village who was supposed to be released and sent home. Why crucify him?

An elegantly dressed woman appeared from behind the back of the judgment seat, leaned over the arm, spoke into Pilate's ear, and retreated as quickly as she came.

Pilate stood and the throng quieted. "In honor of your pious observance, I will release one man to you. I will release the Nazarene."

The words no sooner came out of his mouth than the cries resumed. "Crucify! Crucify!"

From the far side of the court a name was shouted, and within moments everyone was shouting, "Barabbas! Barabbas! Release Barabbas!"

Pilate looked over at the woman who stood in the shadow of the judgment seat. With a perplexed expression, Pilate motioned to a servant, who rushed to his side and placed a bronze basin on the chair's arm. He lifted a large porcelain pitcher and poured water into the basin with an attentiveness that said spillage could be fatal.

With his hands in the water, Pilate looked over his shoulder with disdain. "So be it. You will have your way. Crucify him."

The mob roared its approval, and I sank to my knees. How could this happen? I sobbed. I stood and wiped away the tears. I frantically waved my hands and stretched upward shouting, "No! No! Wait! Please! No!"

But my words were lost in the chaos while the crowd moved around me. Oh, Mama. I glanced over my shoulder. Forcing my way through the horde like a madman, I pushed my way to the bench. The moment Mama and Mariam came into view, I knew they had heard it all.

Mariam buried her head in Mama's chest and wept. Mama, with tears streaming down her cheeks, stared off toward the Praetorium. Her eyes expressed something more, something I couldn't understand. Curiously, the day's events did not appear to take her by surprise—as if she had walked this dark path before.

I knelt, put my arms around them both, and embraced them. Together we wept.

The crowd quieted when a voice shouted in the distance. "They're coming out. They're coming out." Every head turned toward the voice, and each person shuffled away.

Soon Mama, Mariam, and I sat alone in an open corridor across from the entrance to the Stone Pavement where the fanatical expression of injustice had played out. I felt helpless, exhausted of any reason or answer, emptied of any remnant of hope.

With Mama's face in my hands, I looked deep into her eyes. They reflected a combination of anguish and resolution. A heartbreak I would never experience and a comprehension I couldn't fathom.

"Stay here," I said. "I will get us water."

I took a small jug from my rucksack and went to find a cistern. A short distance away, angry voices shouted vulgarities. It was clear who their loathing was fixed upon.

Why did they hate him? He simply proclaimed a view with which the religious leaders and others disagreed. Was that worthy of death? What had he done to justify such anger and hatred?

I'd heard stories, unbelievable stories, of miraculous wonders he had performed. Those closest to him told me he fed multitudes of hungry people with next to nothing. Some said he healed the sick and the lame and even raised some from the dead. Stories. Only stories, I was sure. Even if there was some element of truth, why must he die? Pilate himself had found no reason to put my brother to death.

When I returned with water, Mama and Mariam were standing together at the opening of the wall that led onto Pilate's Stone Pavement. They looked smaller, a little more delicate.

"We must go to where they have taken him," Mama said.

With a weak plea, I said, "Mama, you shouldn't be there."

"We must go. I must be with my son."

A painful, familiar twinge ran through my heart but quickly faded. I was also her son. But, I scolded myself, she was about to lose her firstborn. I put my arm around her trembling frame, took Mariam's hand, and began our passage toward Golgotha.

We stood quietly at the end of a stone path that led to the mound's summit. A crowd had formed, blocking our view, but I made no effort to get any closer. I knew what was taking place, and there was no need for Mama or Mariam to witness it. A scream pierced my heart as the sound of a hammer's blow resonated in the air. I knew that cry.

Shouts of approval and the sounds of weeping erupted as a cross was raised above the crowd. Mama pulled her hand away and disappeared into the throng, followed closely by Mariam. I began to move and was quickly stopped by the bodies that enfolded them. After several minutes of fighting my way through the mass of bodies, I stood looking up into the face of unimaginable pain.

In a moment of agony, he slowly lifted his head and looked at Mama. "Woman, behold your son. Son, behold your mother."

His words humbled me. To know that in such anguish he brought comfort to our mother and to me. I looked up. But his gaze was not fixed upon me, nor were his words intended for me. He'd focused on one of his followers, and upon him Jesus bequeathed the care and responsibility of our mother.

My mind shifted from reason to rage. I was her son, not that beleaguered fisherman. What right did he have to pass on the care of our mother to someone else? I became responsible for her three years ago due to his unwarranted departure. Despite the horror that rose before me, anger resonated within my heart.

Suddenly, the ground under me moved. Disoriented, I grasped the bottom of the cross to steady myself and a warm sensation passed over my hand—my brother's blood. I looked up as his body wrenched in agony, and my anger faded into guilt and shame.

He raised his eyes to heaven and cried out, "It is finished!" Then he closed his eyes and dropped his head. Within a heartbeat I heard the rasp of his final breath leave his body.

Finished? What was finished?

For an inexpressible, inexcusable moment I disregarded his suffering and my mother's torment. I thought only of myself and did the only thing left for me to do. I ran. Like a wounded animal desperate for asylum, I ran. I abandoned my obligation as a son, my bond as a brother, and my responsibility as a man.

I left Mama and Mariam there, at the foot of his cross.

At the worst possible moment.

I fell a short distance away, glancing back just in time to see a centurion step forward and drive a spear into Jesus's side.

✐

Thunder, deep and commanding, drew me back to the tree where I sat. My heart felt as twisted and misshapen as its trunk.

Several of those who had come to see the spectacle of Rome's justice fulfilled began to leave the gruesome scene, walking through my olive treed sanctuary. Their comments about how each of the three thieves received what was due them rang in my ears.

Jumping to my feet I screamed, "You don't know him!" Then I turned and ran, seeking a new, unpopulated harbor in which to hide.

My brother was dead, and I had abandoned him.

"What shall I do, then, with Jesus who is called the Messiah?"
Pilate asked. They all answered, "Crucify him!"
Matthew 27:22

CHAPTER TWO
A Divine Purpose

Crouched among the rocks that overlooked the perimeter wall of the great city, I gazed across the horizon toward what had once been an insignificant mound of earth. The air, dry and sultry, compelled me to take short, shallow breaths to moisten my mouth. In what seemed to be only minutes, the sun became the victim of a heavy blanket of dark clouds that trapped the heat of the day like a lid on a boiling pot.

The sky danced with flashes of light, and a breeze of sultry air blew a chill through me. I drew my legs close to my chest, rested my chin on my knees, and rocked to the rhythm of the funeral dirge that beat in my heart. I prayed that none of the day's events had actually happened, that I was trapped in a hideous dream. Such hope faded when a bolt of lightning illuminated the afternoon sky. A deep rumble of thunder ensued, growling my name like a familiar voice.

In the distance stood the entrance to Herod's Gate in the west wall, where hundreds, perhaps thousands, of figures scurried about. Each was preparing for the continued observance of the Passover celebration—a time to bask in pious traditionalism and rejoice in yesterday's victories, to gather and tell stories of the redemption of God's people.

What unfolded before me extinguished any reason to celebrate. The familiar joy of the Passover season eluded me when Roman centurions marched arrogantly through the streets. They displayed little concern for anyone in their path as they pushed and shoved their way through the congested mass of people.

I scanned beyond the borders of the wall and looked upon what I hoped would not be there. Against the backdrop of thick clouds, the lightning illuminated the sky with a surreal aura, silhouetting a hill, the place where my brother died.

A desolate spot along the road, just outside the Damascus Gate, provided the seclusion I needed. I sat, peered into the darkness, and let my mind drift back to better days. In the cool evenings when storm clouds covered the sky, Jesus and I would walk along the Nazareth Ridge and watch the heavens erupt in a cascade of light. We challenged one another to see who could toss the most rocks off the ridge in the void between the lightning and the thunder. I took great pride in my winning record, but when I grew older, I realized most of my victories had been gifts.

I now waited for the inevitable clap of thunder. In the distance, a rumble swelled and reverberated through the heavens, followed by another barrage of lightning.

I rocked and waited like a child eager for the thunder that follows the lightning. Could I have stopped Jesus's needless death? Should I have taken a stronger stand or spoken out sooner—perhaps when he started all this madness?

⚬⟨∞⟩⚬

The first rays of sunlight signaled the dawn of another day. I turned toward the darkened crevice of the wall and pushed myself deeper into the warmth of my mat. The muffled sounds of children playing and the musky odor of the damp wool draped over my face welcomed me into the morning. In the background came the rhythmic thump of a wooden mallet against a chisel that beat out a melody all its own.

An all-too-familiar voice broke the tranquility of the middle ground between coma and consciousness. "Get up, you lazy pup. We have to make a delivery for Papa before breakfast."

Why is it when you find that perfect spot—where the blankets and mat seem to comfortably harmonize with your body—something needs to be delivered?

"If we don't go now, we won't get back in time to eat. Let's go."

"Okay, okay," I protested. With the corner of my tunic, I wiped away the sleep from my eyes and forced them to confront the light of day.

My eleven-year-old brother was always awake before everyone else and was always cheery. Not me. I knew I looked like a bag of camel hair, and I certainly felt like it.

In hopes of a reprieve I said, "Where are we going, and why do we both have to go?"

Jesus could have gone by himself. He'd done it before. Besides, an important appointment with my good friend Bed and his brother Blanket awaited me.

"Papa wants us to deliver the saddle he repaired," Jesus said.

Even I was surprised at how quickly I readied myself to go. For a long time, I had wanted to see the inside of one of those Roman camps, to know if all the stories were true. The way I figured it, the best way to find out was to go and see for myself. Boy, would my friends be impressed when I told them I had been to the very place we often talked about.

Rome had established a large garrison at Kibbutz, in the valley of Megiddo, seventeen miles from Nazareth. We often walked a mile and sat along the ridge overlooking the valley. From there we could see the dust rise when the Thracian horsemen went out on patrols. At night the campfires across the valley floor sparkled like stars across the night sky. Fortifications ranged from as few as eight to as many as a thousand. The Romans established them along every main road to create a line of defense between upper and lower Galilee. The Zealots had become aggressive, their attacks on Roman encampments increased, and they set up outposts in every village. Rome, in turn, reinforced its position, and Caesar's soldiers could be seen everywhere you looked.

Although the Roman military's need for a craftsman was good for Papa's business, he was careful not to take too much work from them. He did not want anyone in the village to think we gave any support to these heathen oppressors.

The saddle belonged to a Roman soldier who had fallen from his horse in pursuit of a band of robbers near Mt. Carmel. When he fell, his foot caught in the stirrup, and he was dragged along a dried creek bed. Both of his legs had been broken, and he was taken to a camp just outside our village. Because the soldiers were known to treat Jewish women harshly, Papa stayed close to home.

I stepped into the bright morning sun and let my eyes adjust. The smell of burnt wood mixed with the sweet aroma of fresh baked bread arose from the fired bricks of the oven in the center of the court. Mama sorted through some fruits and vegetables, separating those she'd sell from those she'd cook for us.

In the corner near the loom sat Mariam with her perpetual smile and a delightful twinkle in her eyes. Her hands wrapped firmly around the shaft of the grinding stone, patiently turning wheat into meal. This was her part of preparing the meal, freeing Mama to make a new batch of bread. They had been up for hours. A twinge of guilt ran through me but passed quickly. No matter what time of the day, or what chore she did, Mariam glowed with peace and certainty. I walked over and placed my hand on her shoulder. "Thank you, little sister."

At Papa's workshop, I stopped at the doorway and strained to pull back the heavy skins that kept the moisture from the wood. After some effort to make a small opening, I slipped silently through. Inside, I approached the strongest man I knew. My papa. Jesus stood next to him as Papa lifted a large piece of acacia wood and examined its edge. A few finishing touches remained to complete the table—a project made precisely to the instructions given by the elders of the local synagogue. Papa's skilled hands drew the sharp, arched blade of an adze along the wood's edge. No other carpenter in the region could match his craftsmanship. And few men possessed the eye or the strength to hew wood to such perfection.

Papa did not change his position or let go of the wood, but he extended a large, calloused hand in our direction. Although my brother was senior to me, he stepped back and allowed this to be my time. I moved to Papa's side, where he wrapped his strong arm around me and pulled me close. He squeezed me until I thought I would burst.

This was the moment I liked best each morning. His embrace validated his love for me, an affirmation of my importance to him. He released his grip, and I stepped back. Jesus filled the void I left at Papa's side. I reverently held these special moments of personal attention in my mind.

"Keep the saddle covered as you go to the encampment," Papa said. "Don't explain what you are doing to anyone. Our neighbors will not understand why we are making deliveries there." He focused a stern look of loving concern at Jesus. "You know the law. Look after your brother. He can be impetuous."

Sometimes Jesus took his responsibilities too seriously. With the best somber, almost stoic voice an eleven-year-old could muster, he said, "Yes, Papa, I will take good care of him."

Papa strapped the saddle onto a short staff, wrapped a piece of sheep skin on each end, and lifted it onto our shoulders. He pulled back the skins that covered the door, patted us each on the head, and issued a final word of instruction. "Return quickly. Do not collect any payment. I will take care of that later."

A surge of excitement welled up inside me while we journeyed toward the outer border of the village. On the path that led to the Roman encampment, my anticipation grew. I imagined standing among the soldiers we had heard spoken of so often. My imagination built images of statuesque men arrayed in garments of polished brass and exquisite dyed leather.

I envisioned them executing their disciplined drills to ready themselves for war on a faraway battlefield with battering rams, catapults, and ballistae. Their trumpets glistened in the morning sun while the steady beat of drums provided a rhythmic cadence for the soldiers to march to. I imagined the brilliant colors of the raised standards held high when they practiced their maneuvers. The stables were filled with gold and silver chariots that signified the royalty and authority of a Roman cohort. Amid my dream, reality returned by way of Jesus's good-natured cuff to my ear. Oh the stories I would tell my friends later that day.

My excitement soured into fear when we cleared the crest and the encampment came into view. I had only been near a Roman soldier once. I bumped into one in the crowded Jerusalem streets when our family went to celebrate the Passover. I didn't believe the stories the older boys told, but if they were true, I might find myself used for target practice soon.

As we drew closer, my fear turned to curiosity and then faded into disappointment. No walls or embattlements. A few horses were hobbled and set out to pasture to the right of the path. With their scruffy winter coats, swayed backs, and exposed ribs, they weren't the mighty steeds I had expected. There were no glimmering chariots or iron-clad battle wagons—just two rusted-out carts, one on its side and the other missing a wheel. Some soldiers stooped under the burden of water jugs and rolled supply bundles while others milled about. The men looked worn, tired, and broken. They seemed to move aimlessly from one place to another.

A lone guard sat on a stump at the entrance of the encampment, his helmet tilted back, which made his head look like a split grape. A javelin rested across his lap, and a short sword was strapped snug against his side. At his feet lay a breastplate, dull and distorted from abuse. His hands braided long strips of worn cloth into the holes of a forged metal bit.

For the first time since our journey began, my knees buckled under the weight of the load. Not because of the burden we bore but because of the stains in the fabric he knotted together. Blood. Was this the scarlet remnant of a life prematurely snuffed out by a Roman lance or the stained residue of an inattentive cook? I dwelled upon the latter.

We stood patiently for the guard to give us his attention, and after several minutes, Jesus, no longer willing to be ignored, stepped in front of him. In a tone somewhere between command and greeting, he said, "We are here to see Alexander."

Without looking up, the guard said, "What do you want with him?"

"We are returning his saddle."

With a disgusted grunt, the soldier rolled off the stump and stood, letting his javelin fall to the ground. He tossed the bridle at the stump and, without making eye contact, wandered into the camp.

"Are we to follow him?" I said.

"No," Jesus said, "we are Hebrews, and it is against our law for a Jew to associate with or visit a Gentile."

Fine with me. Unlike what I imagined, there was nothing of interest here.

With the staff and saddle set on our shoulders, I took a couple sidesteps and sat on the stump the guard left empty. Jesus sensed my ease and looked back at me. "Do not underestimate these men," he said. "They are men of war, and they are in a foreign land. Don't let the gaze of your eyes put your body in a place of potential peril. Now help me put this down."

I stood and, with care, put the saddle on the stump and gently covered it with the skin. If anyone had watched us, they would have thought we were delivering eggs.

"The soldier who owns this saddle was named after a great king. He must be a man of special quality," Jesus said.

"Was he named after a great king like David? Or after one of the kings of Judah?" I said, as the images I created when Papa taught us of the judges and kings of Israel bounced around in my head.

"No," Jesus said. "Alexander was the great king of Macedonia, whose kingdom God allowed to spread throughout the world."

My disappointment faded when I envisioned the great man I was about to meet. Moisture gathered at the palm of my hands at the thought of the encounter. I turned my attention to the entrance of a large, ornate tent erected in the center of the camp, about forty paces from where we stood. Impatient, I paced, anticipating the appearance of a soldier like that of a mighty warrior king.

A small band of partly armor-clad troops exited the tent and moved under the compulsion of an unseen, silent commander. With the excitement of a funeral dirge, they gathered at the entrance of a smaller shelter to the right of the big tent. Each man exhibited the fruits of war. They wore blood-stained rags. Tattered patches covered eyes that would never again behold a sunrise. Arms that embraced loved ones were gone, and what had been muscular limbs now drew their strength from tightly bound splints.

Two men, with all body parts still attached, grimaced when they lifted a makeshift cot that contained the contorted form of a boy a few years older than Jesus. He lay on his side with his face pushed into a small blanket under his head. The sudden movement of the cot caused him to cry out and shudder. His white-knuckled hands gripped the sides of the cot with such fierceness I thought the flimsy supports would surely break. His legs were wrapped and bound together. When the men who carried the cot approached us, the boy looked up, and I stared into blue eyes of anguish.

His voice tired and distant, he said, "You wanted to see me?"

"Yes," Jesus said, "we have returned your saddle."

"Saddle? What do I need of a saddle? Do I look like I might still become one of Rome's elite cavalrymen to you?" Through gritted teeth, he pointed to his legs. "Keep the saddle. I no longer have use for it. They are taking me to the fortress at Kibbutz to remove these useless limbs. I will have no legs to walk with, let alone place into stirrups." He turned his face into the rough dirty pad of the cot.

Jesus did the unthinkable.

He stepped forward, then reached out and placed his hand upon the wrappings of the young man's twisted legs.

I took a deep breath, closed my eyes, and prepared to hear the boy cry out. I feared the guard near me would react to his cries, and I expected the sharp point of a lance at my throat.

Instead, I heard my brother say, "We will return the saddle to our father's shop where it will remain until your recovery." When I opened my eyes, I let out a breath. The small caravan of broken bodies moved off along the road.

"What is the matter with you?" I squeaked, my voice choked with fear. "You could have gotten us killed if he had cried out. Besides, if we are not allowed to place our foot upon Roman soil, how is it permissible for you to touch a Roman soldier?"

"Agreed, little brother. What you have said is true, but who created that boy and why? What harm is there in giving comfort to a wounded animal?"

How could he compare a helpless, wounded animal to an armed Roman soldier? Never again would I allow myself to become entangled with his debates over what seemed reasonable.

"Papa has taught us that God created all living things, even the animals. There is no harm in caring for a wounded animal, so long as it chooses not to bite. What I don't understand is why God created Romans, because they do nothing but bite."

Removing the goatskin cover from the saddle, Jesus pointed to the piece of carved wood Papa had molded to match an identical piece on the opposite side. A leather thong threaded its way through holes that ran along the edge of both pieces of the saddle's yoke and drew them tightly together. Though taut, it allowed them to bend in the middle so the saddle could lay smoothly over the horse's back.

"Can you see how Papa's hard work brought together different pieces of wood to serve the purpose of the owner? Roman hands constructed the saddle from Aleppo pine, but it is easily broken when stressed. Papa added wood from the cedars of Lebanon to give it strength and to make it whole again."

"What's that got to do with Romans?"

"God created the pine of Aleppo and the cedar of Lebanon, so when they are bound together a man may be victorious in battle. He also created the Jew and the Roman, so when they are bound together, God may be victorious in our lives."

He put the goatskin over the saddle. "A day is coming, little brother, when Israel will cry out and Rome will respond. Woven together, they will fulfill the prophies of old and provide the way for God and man to be united once again."

Great. I knew less now than when the conversation started. I don't know why I ever asked. I couldn't seem to ever get a straight answer, although I must admit, Jesus never failed to give me a response. Sometimes I found myself reflecting on his words when it was quiet and I was alone.

"Get that thing off my seat and move on," yelled the returning entrance guard.

With the staff on our shoulders, we lifted our load and headed down the path.

"Does this mean we can keep the saddle?" I said, knowing a sale could bring more money than what the soldier would have paid for the repair.

"No," Jesus said. "Its owner will have use for it one day."

"I overheard the two soldiers carrying the cot say he might die before they get to Kibbutz," I said. "And if he does not die, he will certainly lose his legs."

Jesus smiled. In a confident tone, he repeated softly, "Its owner will have use for it again."

An explosion of thunder shook the rocks to either side of me, returning me to the pain of the present. How wrong Jesus had been. When Jew and Roman are brought together, the result is not life or victory—but death. This time, his death.

The irony of the Passover festival angered me—families together around tables to reminisce of past days of slavery while those who continued to enslave us walked the streets outside our doors.

This night of reflection and custom brought little hope. Would our circumstances improve after we consumed three wafers of matzo bread, bitter herbs, haroset, sweet vegetables, egg, and roasted lamb? Memories of bloody door posts that protected the Jews from death seemed senseless. Death surrounded us. Freedom was only a word. To consume symbolic food of days past may provide fleeting hope, but it would not change our circumstances.

Raising my fists toward the darkened skies, I yelled, "Stop!" But claps of thunder smothered my cries. No one cared. They were too busy using ritual to block out their worries—a crop in a parched season left behind, loved ones ill or in pain, labors that required attention, and a nation oppressed by foreign invaders. The focus was on God's past grace, when the children of Israel defeated their enemies, when our nation and its people prospered, and when God made His face known. They immersed themselves in history and ignored the present.

I faced Golgotha as the memory of one of many Passover feasts drifted past my mind's eye. One year, when I was the youngest male child of our house, I asked the first of the four questions of the Seder ritual: Why is this night of Passover different from all other nights of the year?

The question echoed with painful sarcasm in my heart. I fell to my knees and screamed at heaven. "Why? What did he do to deserve this?"

Through blurred, tear-filled eyes, I looked at the place my brother took his last breath. I could make out movement along the narrow path that led to the crown of that despicable hill. One figure, much larger than the rest, moved slowly past stationary shadows. An explosion of brilliant light split the sky above the knoll exposing the figure. It was a centurion, a battle-hardened warrior.

Despite the distance, I believe I made out what looked to be a pained expression when he gazed upward. No longer a boy twisted and broken upon a cot but a man arrayed in the polished armor of Rome's elite cavalrymen, firmly seated upon an old worn saddle.

Then the thunder rolled, and the ground shuddered.

With a loud cry, Jesus breathed his last. The curtain of the temple was torn in two from top to bottom. And when the centurion, who stood there in front of Jesus, saw how he died, he said, "Surely this man was the Son of God!"
Mark 15:37–39

CHAPTER THREE

Face in the Crowd

The seclusion I sought among the rocks seemed more of a prison than a sanctuary. A sense of urgency boiled within me, and without plan or purpose, I leapt to my feet. Like a man possessed, I darted around the obscure outline of the rocks and ran down the hillside toward the dim flickering lights of the city, desperate for companionship. Anyone would do, so long as I was no longer alone.

But my journey came to an abrupt and painful stop when I struck a rock that protruded from a small mound, hitting it just below my right knee. With an agonizing cry, I tumbled partway down the hill.

Above me the sound of laughter, deep sarcastic laughter, permeated the air. I rolled onto my back. The blackened clouds rumbled their judgment, and the lightning flashed its applause of agreement.

I inspected my leg for any sign of blood. Relieved to find none, I pulled myself to my feet and hobbled down the hill.

The towers at the four corners of the Fortress of Antonia were easily identifiable and guided me through the darkness to the safety of the North Wall and into a fraternity of pilgrims in an assortment of temporary abodes. Miniature communities grew like wheat upon every flat spot within 120 paces of the city wall. Families huddled together under makeshift shelters, frightened by the unnaturally blackened skies. Consoling one another and their crying children, they stared into the heavens. The clouds continued to erupt in flashes of light and crashes of thunder.

Absorbed into the swarm of humanity, I moved along the path that surrounded the walled city and was soon immersed in the thing I sought—human contact. The humidity that radiated from the tight congestion intensified and overwhelmed me. Every breath became a conscious effort, yet the pain in my leg demanded attention. I protected my injury and worked my way toward the North Gate, searching for a place to rest. To the left of the entrance, secluded in the shadow of one of the great towers, a lone figure sat against the wall.

I pushed my way through the crowd and fell against the wall with a groan of relief. Pressing my back against the stones, I slid to the ground and massaged my wounded limb. I glanced over at the outline of the lone figure in the shadows. I wanted to be around others but did not desire conversation; however, since it was the Passover, I said, "Shalom."

The man remained motionless, his back against the wall and his eyes fixed on the dust of the ground.

Well enough. No response necessary. All I required was his silent presence.

Bright streaks flashed across the sky with such brilliance that I flinched and hit my head against the wall. The dull throb momentarily drew me away from the pain in my leg.

I closed my eyes and allowed my mind to drift from the discomfort within me and the chaos around me.

∽

"Isn't it beautiful?" Jesus said when Herod's Temple came into view.

It was an object of incredible splendor to behold. The dazzling white marble pillars and gold-covered roofs and walls reflected the afternoon sun. The sight took my breath away. Its majestic position on the highest point in the city allowed for a clear view from any direction and gave the structure an ambiance of aristocracy.

The ribbons of roadway that led to Jerusalem remained congested by groups and caravans, travelers from throughout Palestine and every corner of the Roman Empire. Though most were on foot, some rode donkeys, camels, and even oxen, weighed down with their provisions and offerings. The pilgrims came to fulfill the mandate of Moses: "Every male of every house shall appear before the Lord your God." The rainy season had ended, and the roads that had been rivers of mud had become rivers of life—literal estuaries of activity.

In our home during the Sabbath, Papa taught us of our heritage. He described the great kings, wise judges, and mighty warriors. Images of fantastic kingdoms, beautiful cities, and glorious places of worship would form in my head as he spoke.

But no description could have prepared me for my first sight of Herod's Temple. Like the flow of a river, tens of thousands of people streamed toward the awesome structure.

Two years ago, Jesus had tried to describe its beauty when he and Papa came back after making a delivery to Jerusalem with the men of the village. I struggled to envision what he said, but now I understood. As the oldest sons, we accompanied Papa when he presented our family offering. Papa felt it important we observe and become accustomed to the obligations of Jewish manhood. But I was only ten at the time—there was plenty of time before I would become a man. Jesus, however, would be a man the next year when he turned thirteen.

I had one regret on that trip—I would not be allowed to enter the temple's inner court when the offering was presented.

My siblings and I bore the bulk of our provisions and walked with Mama while Jesus strode ahead with a bantam white lamb leashed tight at his side. The animal jerked and tugged at the rope, bleating protest as if it knew its fate. Jesus treated this lamb like a child.

He had found the little creature in a field of sky-blue flax. The lamb's short white wool stood out in the rich green and blue overgrowth—most likely left behind by a caravan from the East. The newborn creature needed to be hand-fed, a task Jesus reluctantly surrendered to Mariam. Her gentle touch inspired strength in the little creature.

We were all surprised when Jesus suggested the lamb be presented for the Passover offering. Mariam objected with tearful pleas, and we all knew how much Jesus loved the lamb. During our evening devotions, the lamb would curl up beside him, its head in his lap. That little ball of white was always by his side.

"What we tender to God must not be some of what we have but the absolute best we have. Did not King David say he would give nothing to God unless it were a sacrifice? Could we do any less?" Jesus said, echoing Papa's words during our evening devotion about the importance of sacrificial giving.

After several contemplative moments, we all agreed, even Mariam.

In Jerusalem, my youthful ignorance did not prepare me for the tense atmosphere created by the clash of Jewish culture with Roman deployment. Small bands of heavily armed Roman troops stationed themselves in various places along the roadway. Their watchful eyes continued to pan the crowds for any sign of trouble. Tables covered with a kaleidoscope of foods, fabrics, and trinkets lined the path. Hawkers held up their wares and aggressively shouted for our attention. Professional beggars cried out and grabbed at us when we passed, some of their bodies contorted in a way that filled me with pity. Mariam drew closer to Mama's side, a place I envied.

We stopped at the Pool of Bethesda near the Temple Mount. Jesus entered the pool and, according to strict ceremonial requirements, cleansed himself so he might enter holy ground. At first, I was embarrassed and rather shy, until I saw how seriously my brother approached this ritual. With reverence, I followed his example. A sense of renewal washed over me when I stepped into the waters for my first ritual bath. I felt clean—cleaner than I ever felt before.

Quickly we dried, dressed, and left so others could take our place. We passed over a viaduct and through the shadow of the great arch of the Sheep Gate and entered the Court of the Gentiles—a piazza large enough to hold a city. Yet we were swallowed up by the mob that had gathered. The sound of countless accents and foreign tongues filled our ears with incomprehensible babble. We held close to one another and moved toward the low stone wall that encircled the temple's inner courts.

I tugged on Jesus's arm and pointed at the words inscribed on the wall in Greek and Latin. "What does it say? I can only make out a few of the words."

"No foreigner," he read, "may enter within the balustrade and enclosure around the temple area. Anyone caught doing so will bear the responsibility for his ensuing death."

A chill fluttered in my heart when we passed through the stone balustrade and climbed the steps surrounding the temple domain.

The atmosphere took on a refreshing change when we entered the Court of Women. In various places in the center of the court, exhorts stood on elevated small platforms and proclaimed visions of divine truth. Symposiums of scribes and scholars gathered under awnings and debated points of religious concept. Here Jews seemed more open and outspoken about the coming messiah and the ultimate defeat of Rome. Was such dialogue the cause of the nervous expressions upon the faces of the soldiers who stood guard outside the three gates?

"Come here, son," Papa said. From the pouch at his side, he withdrew a Tyrian silver half shekel and handed it to me. "Every Jewish man must pay his temple tax." He smiled.

I turned to my brother and saw acceptance and pride in his eyes. I located the farthest of the thirteen treasury chests, each shaped like a ram's horn. I took the hem of my tunic, spit on the coin, and rubbed it so hard I thought the engraved image might come off. I wanted to run to the offering chest, but instead I pranced across the marble floor, aware that many eyes watched me. I held out my hand so the sun glimmered off my offering, and I savored the moment with each step.

Short of the offering chest, I waited impatiently for my turn behind several men who continued to search through their pouches for a coin. In front of me stood a boy who did not appear to be much older than me. I stretched upward and stood on my toes to appear taller. Shoulders back and chest out, I spoke in a voice that came from someplace near my sandals. "Shalom."

"Shalom," the boy said.

"Presenting your offering too?" I said, casually looking away, trying to put on an air of boredom with the routine.

"Yes," he said in a haughty tone.

"Me too." I shrugged.

After each man presented his offering and the path cleared, I stepped up to the chest and let my coin drop with enough force to make a solid ringing sound, in case someone had missed my presence. With all the manliness I could muster, I turned and walked confidently away.

Upon my return, Mama greeted me with open arms and gave me a hug. "I'm so proud of you," she said. Her eyes glistened with unshed tears.

"Mariam and I will wait for you here," she said. "We are not allowed to go any farther than this. Stay close to your brother and father."

We ascended the fifteen curved steps to the Nicanor Gate and stopped short of the long narrow stone pavement of the Court of the Israelites. Through the gate I saw into the Court of the Priests and the high altar with its four horn-shaped corners. No metal tool could touch any of the stones, so the altar had a rough, unfinished appearance. This stood in stark contrast to the smooth finish of the rest of the temple. The air was blanketed with smoke and the odor of blood, incense, and charred animal fat. Conversations, prayers, and praise rose in harmony with the bleats, groans, and chirps of lambs, rams, goats, doves, pigeons, and cattle. A chorus only God could appreciate.

"Will we be able to see the actual sacrifice?" I whispered into Jesus's ear.

"Yes," he said, his voice tight with emotion. Putting his hand on my shoulder, he moved me closer to the archway, against the hinge of the great door. From there, I had a clear view of the altar. He bent down, lifted his lamb into his arms, and buried his face into its wool.

"What's the matter with him?"

I turned to see the boy whom I met in the Court of Women.

"The lamb that will be offered means a great deal to him."

"So what? Doesn't he know it is a great honor just to be in the temple during Passover? Not to mention the privilege to have his offering presented by a priest."

"Yes, but it's hard when you know something you love will be put to death."

The strong arm of my brother anchored itself around my shoulder, and he pulled me to his side.

"Someone better explain to him what a sacrifice is," said the young man behind me. "That's what they do here you know."

My body stiffened and Jesus tightened his grip. "This is neither the time nor the place, little brother. Besides, he's right."

Right. How could he say that? This part of his character irritated me. Not only would he ignore an offense, but he saw worth in every offender. My anger faded when the sound of reed pipes filled the air, and the temple Levites sang from the Psalms. A long row of priests, each with a bowl made of gold and silver, formed a line to the altar. Papa extended his hand to Jesus, who stepped forward and handed him the lamb.

Papa entered the gate, passing through the Court of the Israelites and into the Court of the Priests. At the first row of priests, he was handed a sharp knife. He turned just enough to look back, catch Jesus's eye, and give a slight nod. Jesus responded with a nod of understanding and compliance. Swiftly, before the lamb became aware of any danger, Papa opened its neck and allowed the blood to empty into the priest's bowl. The bowl passed from priest to priest until it reached the base of the altar. There the last priest in line emptied the bowl upon the altar, allowing the blood to splash and pour down its sides. A temple worker took the body of the young lamb, prepared it for the Seder, and returned it to Papa.

"I will carry this for you, Papa," Jesus said as he took the remains of the lamb.

"Your pet received a great honor as the paschal lamb for our village. Do you understand the importance of that?" Papa said, his eyes moist.

"Yes," Jesus said quietly. "I know a sacrifice is necessary."

My reflection was interrupted by an abrupt and deafening clap of thunder, along with a resurgence of pain in my leg. Someone had just kicked my injured limb. I rolled onto my side, dragged my leg up into my arms, and held my breath to avoid screaming. I spotted the culprit who had assaulted my battered limb—a small boy being dragged along by his mother.

From my prone position, I could see that my companion in the shadows took no notice of this unexpected intrusion; he did not even lift his face from his hands. At first, I thought he had fallen asleep or was just oblivious to what took place on around him. I wondered if he was dead. Then his body convulsed with uncontrollable weeping. Had he experienced a loss as severe as mine? As odd as it may seem, this stranger's pain comforted me. I felt less alone in my sorrow and pain. I pulled myself back up against the wall. After the pain subsided a bit, I attempted to greet him again. "Shalom. Peace be with you, friend."

Slowly he lifted his head and turned toward me, his eyes red and swollen.

His eyes spoke of wonders and disasters, hope and loss. Yet they also reflected a strange, familiar glint. Without a word, he turned away from me and stared into the darkness. The lightning etched the outline of his profile.

I knew him. I was sure of it, but from where?

"I know you," I said.

He jumped to his feet, rushed past me, and picked up speed.

"Wait, I know you. Wait."

He fled like a man pursued by his greatest fears. His movements were purposeful, as if something drove him forward toward a specific goal.

Although my leg throbbed, I lifted myself up and attempted to follow him, but my movements were impeded by pain.

"Please wait," I cried out. "I wish to speak with you."

Before he melted into the mass of bodies, he turned and looked back at me. An explosion of light covered the sky, and a simultaneous crash of thunder shook the ground. His face contorted, as if he wanted to cry out for help—or perhaps forgiveness. Whatever the reason for his haste, the look of unmistakable resignation was clear. There was a destination that awaited him, a objective he had to reach.

He knew me as sure as I knew him. I had met him in the temple during another Passover. He was one of my brother's followers.

With one last grand effort, I shouted at the top of my voice, "Wait, Judas! Please wait!"

When Judas, who had betrayed him, saw that Jesus was condemned, he was seized with remorse and returned the thirty pieces of silver to the chief priests and the elders. "I have sinned," he said, "for I have betrayed innocent blood." "What is that to us?" they replied. "That's your responsibility." So Judas threw the money into the temple and left. Then he went away and hanged himself.
Matthew 27:3–5

CHAPTER FOUR

Choice of Destiny

Leaning against the city wall, I limped along as the heavens again exploded in brilliant light. The skies seemed angry about the day's events. Through eyes blurred by sorrow, I watched the silhouetted figures disappear from Golgotha's hill. The curious and the coldhearted must have lost sadistic interest in watching men die. Were they returning to the comfort of their camps, families, and friends to sit around the fire and weigh in on the merits of Roman rule?

On this Passover Eve, these assessors of justice would make preparations meant to commemorate God's merciful intervention even as they judged those whose lives ended on the rocky hill nearby.

The pain in my leg took my mind off the pain in my heart. Looking up, I searched the dark afternoon sky for any glimmer of hope that would bring a little light into the midst of my despair. Finding none, I slumped back into the darkness. Anger welled up within me as I imagined the chatter flowing from self-opinionated judges around the evening fires. Certainly they would discuss the merits of crucifixion—a Roman method of public execution that max-imized pain and humiliation.

I had sat around such fires and enjoyed the warmth of self-righteous blather. Some would speak of the cruelty of the cross and focus on the brutality of the executioners, but they would be few. Most would ignore the Romans' callous assassins and support the use of the cross as a necessary means of eliminating social pariahs, such as murderers and, of course, thieves.

The thieves. What could a thief possibly steal to deserve such a horrific death? A scrap of bread? A frayed cloak? Besides, what right did any of the observers have to debate a man's guilt or innocence? What did they know? Their arro-gant fault-finding made them as guilty of violating the heart of God as those thieves hanging at my brother's side.

Looking down at the dirt, I mulled over my thoughts. When had I become so virtuous that I could adjudicate the words and lives of others? Wasn't I the one who ran when the world turned dark? I should have never abandoned those closest to me when they felt his pain and their hearts broke.

Tucking myself as tightly as I could into a dark corner along the wall, I looked out toward that abominable hill. My mind floundered in murky pools of shame and regret. What had I done? More importantly, what hadn't I done?

It was Passover. A time when every man's mission was to come to Jerusalem and worship, to bring sacrifices for atonement, and to celebrate. But I had come with a different mission. I came to retrieve. To again rescue my elder brother from his emotional and irresponsible desire to change the world.

Our small band—Mama, Mariam, and I—began our trek to Jerusalem believing it would be a brief repeat of past undertakings. We would locate Jesus, retrieve him, and conclude our journey with a family Passover celebration. We then would return home with our wayward sibling, and life would be normal again.

How wrong we were.

A blaze of intense light ripped through the darkness, striking the ground a few paces in front of me. Dirt and rocks flew in every direction. My mind reeled as the air flexed and became phosphorescent, sparking and crackling as if it were alive. The blast drove me back against the cold stone wall, forcing the breath from my lungs. A pungent odor of what smelled like burnt wool flooded my nostrils, then everything went black.

⌘

Returning with a small vial of olive oil and a roll of cloth exchanged for at the local market, Mariam and I watched the sun retreat below the horizon, its work done for another day. On the ridge overlooking Nazareth, I stopped. "Mariam, go home and tell Papa I'll be home shortly." As a teenage boy, time alone, away from family, was a luxury.

"You know Papa doesn't like it when you're out alone. It's not safe," she said.

"I'll be all right. Tell Mama I'll bring more wood too."

As she reached the crown of the knoll, I anticipated the glance over her shoulder—the worried look she always gives me when she leaves me. Reaching the crest, she slowed, turned, and studied me. This time her expression was not simple concern for a brother who no doubt was going to get in trouble with Papa but one of real apprehension.

Mariam was always aware when something was amiss. She had an inner sensitivity that told her when things weren't right. She believed God had given her an innate knowledge that helped her to discern future events, particularly bad ones. She called it her "understanding." She did not like the awareness; during evening prayers, she often asked God to take it from her.

I waved her on reassuringly, knowing that sending her home on her own would make Papa angry. But we were close to home, and besides, if I brought extra wood, that might ease his anger. I was getting older, and Papa always taught us to stand on our own.

I found a comfortable spot and watched as the orange, yellow, and blue faded from the earth's edge. At first the stars were only slight flickers in the night sky; then they began to sparkle like a king's treasure. Looking heavenward, I marveled at God's handiwork and wondered why he had made such beauty. When Papa honed olivewood smooth and polished it to a fine luster, he did so for a reason. Nothing was wasted. Every effort, every stroke of his adze, served a purpose. What did God have in mind when he placed the stars in the sky? What was their purpose?

"What are you doing out here, little brother?" Jesus's voice pierced the darkness.

"I just wanted to spend some time alone," I said with emphasis on the last word.

He placed his hand on my shoulder and gazed upward. "Beautiful isn't it?" After a brief silence, he said, "When King

David was a boy your age, he spent most of his nights alone, looking at those same lights and talking with God."

Jesus often said things like that as if he had been there when it happened. Looking up, I wondered if King David ever questioned God. In his prayers, did he ever ask God to let him be more than a shepherd? I certainly wanted to be more than a carpenter.

Lifting his hand from my shoulder, Jesus stepped in front of me. "God made everything in our wonderful world, little brother, and he gave it to us to enjoy." Looking down at me with that look Papa gets when he was about to teach me something or correct me, he said, "You cannot choose where the stars have been placed, but you can choose where you will be when they come out and illuminate your path."

"What does that mean?"

"King David made many choices both before and after he became king. He could have remained in the fields, but instead he chose to follow God's leading. That's what we read in the Tanakh in the synagogue."

"I know," I said, annoyed by his authoritative tone. "I've heard all the stories." All I wanted at that moment was to be left alone with my own thoughts.

Dropping his head, he said with a tone of sadness, "God gave David the same stars and the same opportunities you have, little brother. King David made many wise choices, but sometimes his choices were not the right ones." Stepping back, he met my gaze. "We don't read about those in the synagogue."

As quietly as he came, he walked away. "Don't be late," he said, disappearing into the darkness.

Sometimes I just didn't grasp what Jesus was saying. Although I believed what he said was right—his words felt true—it often seemed he meant more than he said.

Alone again, I lay on my back and stared at the flickering night sky, drifting into a realm of imaginary challenges. But my dreams ended abruptly when I was jarred back to reality by a slap to my forehead. "Hey, what are you doing out here?"

Tilting my head backward, I looked up at a dirty face with two missing front teeth. "I'm waiting for some friends," I said. That wasn't exactly true, but Dismas wasn't known for being truthful, so stretching the truth seemed fitting.

"I have an idea, and you are the perfect one to help me with it." He gave me a broad grin.

Dismas was older by a few years, and he was able to go where he wanted, whenever he wanted. No one told him what to do or when to be home. "Let's find Gestas," he said. "We'll need him too."

After walking a short distance from the main road, we came to a small settlement just outside the village of Ofel. I had known Gestas and Dismas for several years. I had met them in the village and knew they were both refugees, but I knew little else and had never met their families or been to their homes. Around a small campfire sat Gestas, eating. On either side sat an older disheveled man and an ample-formed woman, dipping bread into a bowl. These, no doubt, were his mother and father. Next to them crouched three children, probably his siblings. But I couldn't tell whether his siblings were boys or girls. Their hair was all the same length, their faces covered in grime, and their clothing badly worn. The family looked as if they hadn't bathed since the last rain, and we hadn't had rain for months. The fires in the cooking pits cast a surreal reflection of shadows that danced along their tattered tents.

Remaining in the shadows, Dismas shouted, "Gestas!"

The family sprang to their feet, and the children scampered to the tent with their mother close behind. The older man grabbed a large staff lying near his feet and stepped toward us. "What do you want?" The look on his face and the tone in his voice caused me to stand still.

"Gestas. We've come to see Gestas," Dismas said with what sounded like a quiver in his voice. Gestas remained seated, staring out into the darkness in our direction.

"What do you want with him?" the old man barked.

"We're friends. We just wanted to—"

"Go away." The man raised his staff in the air and yelled, "Gestas has no friends."

Panic rose in my throat because I knew I was about to meet the knobby end of the old man's staff.

Taking hold of my arm, Dismas pulled me back. "Let's go."

Stepping around the fire pit, Gestas called to us, "Wait." Pushing the old man aside, he joined us as we walked away.

"You know what will happen when you come back!" the old man shouted.

I turned and saw absolute rage on his face. Behind him two small dirty faces with wide eyes stared out from the folds of the ragged tent as they took refuge behind their mother.

Dismas and Gestas whispered to each other and hurried down the path, leaving me to tag along behind.

"Where are we going?" When they didn't respond, I quickened my pace and asked, "What are we going to do?"

Except for the glitter of distant stars, little light illuminated our way.

As we traveled farther from my home, a furious debate arose in my head. The deep inner voice that usually came as a beckoning whisper resonated like a shout. *I must go home. Now.* But another voice countered: *What will my new friends think? Besides, I'm already in trouble. Papa will have more than a strong rebuke when I get home.*

Keeping track of their outlines and movements, I saw their darkened figures melt into the night as they dropped to the ground.

"Get down," they said when I tripped over their slouched forms.

I was about to ask what we were doing when a grimy hand covered my mouth.

"Quiet," whispered Gestas, hand tightening. "We're here."

A short distance away, a campfire flickered, and shadowy figures moved about in the darkness. Gestas released his grip on my mouth and brought a finger up to his lips. Turning, he crawled toward the encampment, followed by Dismas. Watching them move stealthily away, the voice that warned me of impending doom shrieked, *Danger!* Fear and excitement bubbled in my chest as I battled the desire to crawl forward and the overwhelming urge to stand and run away. Before I could make a reasonable or rational decision, I was skulking behind my cohorts toward the campfires.

Reaching the edge of the camp, I saw what appeared to be a small company of Roman infantry—two reclining near the fire and the others sleeping a short distance away. Behind them, I saw men similar to those Papa and I had encountered once. He told me to be careful of such men and why I should avoid them. These were not battle-hardened centurions but auxiliary recruits, volunteers made up of young men and boys hoping to one day become part of Rome's elite army.

Pointing to the sentries seated near the fire, Dismas said, "We'll wait here until those two are asleep."

"Wait for what?" Lying motionless, I tried to hold my breath. No doubt my friends could hear me breathing—unless the pounding in my chest was louder. What were we waiting for? What were we going to do? I looked over at Gestas, only to find him sleeping. Sleeping! "O Lord, don't let him snore," I prayed silently.

Before long, our intrepid posse stirred. "Come on," Dismas said, pushing Gestas's shoulder. "You wait here," he said, pointing at me.

"I thought you needed my help."

"Not yet." He waved me off.

Had I been demoted? No, it wasn't that they didn't need me. Dismas was protecting me.

The two crept toward the encampment. Reaching the area where the brush was cleared away, they separated and made their way to the recruits' belongings. Their deliberate movements indicated they had done this before.

The purpose of our journey dawned on me like a dark storm. They—no, we—were about to become thieves. My desire to run turned into panic, but any movement was out of the question.

I lost sight of Dismas, but Gestas remained in clear view as he moved methodically, instinctively toward his target. The heads of the two sentries were propped up on shields.

Eyes closed and mouths open, each man covered in a torn, well-worn cape. They weren't sentries because they weren't actually on guard. They were just too tired or too drunk to get up and move with the others.

Remembering what Papa told me about these wannabe centurions caused an even greater fear to rise up. This camp didn't need a sentry because there wasn't anything of value to steal. Besides, no rational person would wander into their camp.

These men were far worse than regular centurions. These were unmanageable outcasts given just enough unrestrained power to be dangerous. Rome used these ruthless scoundrels to clean out pockets of resistance in areas of little importance to the State. No point in wasting trained soldiers to do the work these rabble-rousers could do. They provided inexpensive assistance with a merciless result: their pay came from what they plundered. There I was, offering up myself to their unrestrained depravity at the ripe old age of thirteen.

Gestas rose slightly, surveying the group at the far side of the camp for any movement. Lowering himself again, he cautiously reached toward a haversack lying beside one of the sleeping watchmen. I held my breath as the danger intensified. The other sentry near the fire grunted loudly, rolled onto his side, and pushed aside the robe that covered his head.

Gestas stopped, his arm extended, his hand on the haversack.

Eyes closed, I lay as still and flat as possible. Although I had pushed my face deep into the soft dirt, I heard muffled movement in front of me. Fear kept me motionless. All I could do was pray, and pray I did, fervently.

Jesus once told me God heard all our prayers, even the prayers we said in our minds. I couldn't help but wonder if God heard the silent prayers of a thief in the making, and I was calling out to God with every part of my being. "O Lord, help Gestas not wake anyone as he works his way back to us— after he steals something." What kind of prayer was that?

I opened my eyes and lifted my head. Looking out toward the camp, I saw nothing. Gestas was gone. Panic pumped in my veins. To my horror, the two drunks that slept a few paces away were also gone.

A hand jerked me to one side and pushed me down onto my back. Fear pierced my chest like a sharp lance. As my eyes cleared, a familiar toothless grin came into focus.

"Shhhhh." Dismas leaned in close to my face. "Look what I got," he whispered, holding up a small leather bag. Looking around, he said, "Where's Gestas?"

"I don't know."

Loud voices rose from the other side of the camp. Moving as fast and as silently as possible, we retreated and took refuge under heavy overgrowth a short distance away. Crouching, we peered through the foliage. Two large men appeared from the darkness illuminated by the light of the campfire. Behind them came three more. Two were the intoxicated watchmen who dragged Gestas with such force that he barely touched the ground. Entering the clearing around the camp, they tossed him like a limp rag toward the fire. Hitting the ground with a resounding thud, he scampered away from the flames, scattering burning embers and throwing sparks into the air. Rolling onto his back, he lifted himself onto his elbows.

The light from the fire illuminated Gestas's face clearly enough to reveal the blood running from his mouth and nose—a nose that appeared different. The lambent light also exposed the contemptible glares of his captors. No fear, no panic. I could not discern even the slightest concern in their expressions—just pure, unadulterated hatred.

Lifting a cloth pouch into the air, one of the sentries said, "Is this what you're after?" He struck Gestas across the face with the pouch.

Turning to Dismas and looking down at the small leather bag in his hand, I whispered, "Give it back."

He hissed into my ear, "No. If we show ourselves now, we'll be dead too. There's no need to sacrifice ourselves. Gestas can take care of himself."

Opening the pouch, the sentry poured its contents into his hand and held up two coins that fell out. "You want them, you can have them," he said, tossing the coins into the fire.

No one moved for several moments. The sentry bent over, a hand-breadth from Gestas's face, and bellowed, "What's the matter, boy? There's your money. Get it."

Gestas didn't move toward the fire. He spat blood into the sentry's face. The large man jerked back, took several steps, and fell on his backside.

A second man stepped forward and struck Gestas across the side of the head with a bound bundle of wooden rods used to make the handle of a Roman battleax. Gestas went limp and collapsed on his side. Was he unconscious?

Dismas grunted and shifted his weight as if he were about to stand. I grabbed the sleeve of his robe and shook my head. Settling back down, he hid his face in his hands and sobbed.

Wiping his forehead with the sleeve of his robe, the sentry took the battleax from the man's hands and stood over Gestas, looking down at him as a hunter would look at a wounded animal. Fear for Gestas's life washed over me. Dismas and I both stood when the sentry turned and walked away toward the fire. Squatting back down, we watched as he knelt beside the flames and, using the ax, probed the embers.

"Wake him up." He snorted. The other sentry hovered over Gestas and poured liquid from a clay jug over his head. Jolting upright, Gestas coughed and choked, shivering and shaking his head.

Rising up from the fire with two red-hot coins on his ax blade, the sentry turned, walked back to where Gestas sat, bent down, and sneered. "You want them, you can have them." Two men pushed Gestas onto his stomach. One placed a knee on his back while the other held his head to the ground. The sentry dropped the coins onto Gestas's neck, just below his right ear.

A chilling howl rose as Gestas cried out and struggled to twist free from their grip. The sound of his pain was mixed with laughter from those who watched his agony. The sentry clutched Gestas's robe and tore off a ragged piece as the men released their hold. Reaching down, using the torn fragment, the sentry ripped the seared coins from his neck. "I'll know you if I see you again," he said. "Make sure I do not." Turning, they walked away in the direction of a grassy incline where they had been sleeping.

Gestas slowly lifted himself to his knees and crawled toward us. When he drew near, Dismas broke from our cover and scurried to reach our friend. Putting his arm around Gestas, Dismas crawled back to the shrubs. Moving into a small, well-concealed clearing, Gestas rolled onto his side and lay motionless. Even in the dim firelight, I could see the likeness of Augustus Caesar burned into his neck. We sat in silence until he regained some strength. When he was ready, we walked, then ran. But this time I had no difficulty keeping up with them.

Running in the dark can be treacherous, and in most circumstances, my pace would have been slow and cautious, but not that night. We wanted to put as much space between us and those malcontents as possible. If that meant colliding with a tree branch or getting entangled in brush, then so be it. Avoiding well-worn trails and cutting new routes across dried creeks beds, we found ourselves at the edge of a small settlement of refugees.

Dismas lived there with his father, sister, and little brother. They'd fled from their home in Sidon when Rome recognized the area as a prime commercial port and confiscated their property. The family's move had been a simple decision, Dismas told me. They voluntarily gave all they possessed for the good of Rome or they died.

When we stopped in front of a thatched-roof mud hut, a bearded man stepped out and walked toward us. He spoke in an agitated voice that seemed to shake the ground we stood on. "Where have you been?"

Hesitantly, Dismas held up the small leather bag. "I got this for you."

Snatching it from his hand, the big man grumbled, "What is it?" His meaty fingers fumbled trying to open it. "Better be good." Pouring the contents onto his palm, he looked down, closed his fist, and gestured for Dismas to come closer.

Looking over his shoulder at Gestas, Dismas gave an approving grin and moved to his father's side. The big man turned slightly, shifted his weight, and struck Dismas with such force it knocked him to the ground a couple paces away.

"What do you think I can do with these?" he growled, tossing the pouch on the dirt in front of him. Opening his hand, he dropped three round Roman marbles, one at a time, on Dismas's head.

Looking up at us, his face grimaced in pain, Dismas groaned. "Go. ... Go now. ... Go," he stammered.

Gestas and I ran as if pursued by the devil himself. I glanced back, relieved that the big man wasn't following us. However, what I saw stopped me in my tracks. Dismas didn't move from the spot where he landed. The big man stood over him as Dismas dropped his head and folded his arms in front of him. His father raised a staff he'd retrieved from the side of the mud hut and brought it down sharply across the boy's back. Falling forward from the blow, Dismas lay motionless as his father repeatedly struck him.

"We need to go back," I said, out of breath.

"Are you crazy? His father will kill us," Gestas said. "Dismas can take it."

Reaching a fork in the road, we stopped. I fell on my back and gulped the air. Gestas touched his neck and winced in pain.

"Go home. I'll get Dismas tomorrow night. Meet us here at dusk." Slowly, he walked into the darkness.

I had never taken anything that wasn't mine. But that night I entered the ranks of thieves and robbers, and my compliance earned me an invitation to extend my pilfering career.

I entered the small courtyard of our home where Mariam sat by the door waiting for me. "Papa is really angry," she said.

"How angry?" I said, images of Dismas's father running through my mind.

"Where's the wood?" she said.

Great, I thought. I forgot the appeasement that was going to diffuse Papa's anger.

"You'll have extra chores to do." Mariam said with the sternest look she could muster.

"Extra chores?" I laughed. "Good night, Mariam."

Tumbling onto my cot, I laid on my side facing the wall and listening to the noises of the night. Dogs barking, crickets chirping, frogs croaking, and the family snoring. None of those sounds could drown out the screams echoing in my mind. *What have we done?*

"Go to sleep, little brother." That familiar voice in the dark.

"Is Papa angry with me?" I whispered.

"Yes."

"I saw two angry fathers today," I said, tears welling up. "They were very angry. Very angry." My voice trembled. "Does Papa have a staff? I haven't seen him with one."

"Yes. In his shop beneath the wood pile," Jesus said. "He has no need for it."

Staring into the dark, my mind repainted the night's horror. The burns on Gestas's neck. The rage on Dismas's father's face as he beat his son. Our every move played over and over in my head as Gestas's screams rang in my ears.

"Some do not control their emotions, little brother," Jesus said. "They choose to express rather than control the anger that rises up in their hearts."

How did he know? He wasn't there. "What? What are you talking about?"

"Papa loves you, and he has a staff," he said. "Papa is also angry about the choices you have made. But his anger will not be expressed by his staff."

Rolling over, I said, "What choices? How does Papa know about the choices I've made?"

A long silence filled the air as I pondered the options laid before me that evening and the choices I made. What would tomorrow bring? I didn't know what Dismas and Gestas would choose to do as the sun set tomorrow, but I knew one thing: they would be doing it alone.

"Your father knows the choices you make before you make them. His love for you is greater than his disappointment," Jesus said. After a long, quiet moment he added, "You are no longer a child. The choices you make you must live with, brother." He paused. "As do your friends."

⌘

A low rumble began in the direction of that horrid hill and slowly increased in intensity as it crossed the heavens. Earlier in the day, before we went to Pilate's Pavement, I left Mama and Mariam with friends who lived in the southern quarter and went into the market to retrieve supplies for our return trip home. I was halted at the Damascus Gate by a crowd gathered around an overturned cart, its fruits and vegetables scattered across the entrance. Children scurried around, grabbing all that their little hands could hold. Their parents maneuvered themselves between the owner of the cart and their thieving offspring to conceal their activity. What a fitting way, I thought, to enter the holiest of cities.

A captain of the Centurion Guard watched the chaos and bellowed a command in my direction. When I turned toward the voice, I caught the elbow of a man who moved through the crowd like a jackal about to pounce on its prey. His eye was on a melon that had fallen from the cart and rolled near my feet.

Of sizable girth, he was about to reach for the melon when the guard pushed him with such force that he fell headlong into me. I stumbled backward trying to catch my balance, but both of us went down, catching the clothing of others under our feet and pulling down several would-be fruit pilferers.

Without so much as a downward glance, the centurion stepped over us, dragging several half-naked men tethered by interwoven lengths of twine.

I lay there motionless as they paraded past—heads down, eyes glazed, covered in filth. Every part of their exposed bodies bled from some bruise or wound. They were the dregs—thieves, anarchists, and murders. Despite having already experienced "Roman hospitality," they were on their way to be judged for their misdeeds. Watching them pass, I wondered what evil they had done to justify the torment of the whipping post or of forfeiting a finger, a hand, or their life.

One of these unfortunate dissidents looked familiar, but I couldn't get a good look at his face. When he turned his back to me, I saw he had scars from an old injury on the right side of his neck, just below his ear. There were two circles, one above the other. They were not abrasions but burns—more brands than injuries.

"Gestas!" I yelled. "Gestas!"

He slowed and began to turn toward me when the blunt end of a centurion's spear was jammed into his side. He groaned and stumbled forward when the prisoner in front of him pulled sharply on the rope that bound them together. Grunting, he picked up his pace, blending into the mass of tethered bodies.

Sitting against the wall hours later, I looked out at a rise of earth where three distinct crosses stood. My brother's voice resounded in my head as if he were shouting from a distant shore: "The choices you make you must live with, brother. As do your friends."

A chill crept up my legs. Four crosses could have been erected on that hill had I made different choices. "God's hand is upon my life," I whispered, "but I am free to determine its course. A simple turn can have a profound effect. I could be at my brother's side at this moment, but unlike him, I would be begging for a quick, merciful death."

Although the sky was dark, the crosses remained visible. They rose up from the earth like a repugnant declaration of man's unquenchable craving to devise and improve on how he might inflict suffering on others. There they hung—the guiltless among the guilty, innocence among thieves.

What had Jesus done to deserve such an agonizing, repulsive, degrading death? What choices had brought him here? I knew the choices that Dismas and Gestas had made and the consequences that resulted. My life could have warranted the effects of poor choices, but not Jesus's. Not his.

A blameless man suffered on that hill, and his choices put him there, as innocent as they may have been. Thieves died there as well, and they were culpable. On that hill hung my brother, and at his side hung two of my friends.

Two other men, both criminals, were also led out with him to be executed. When they came to the place called the Skull, they crucified him there, along with the criminals—one on his right, the other on his left.

Luke 23:32–33

CHAPTER FIVE

Place of Comfort

I became an island, a small spot of despair in a sea of confusion. I walked slowly through the arch of the Fish Gate into the frenzied activity of the marketplace. Pilgrims milled about me like the waves of an angry sea, each frantic in their aspiration to fulfill their designated purpose in the Passover celebration. For me, any thought of celebration had been lost in the flood of the day's events.

Working my way through the crowd, I all but dropped onto a small bench near Solomon's Quarries. Massaging my bruised leg, I struggled to muster the strength or even the desire to move on.

Even if I could have summoned the energy, I no longer had a place to go. As the pain in my head and lower leg subsided, the pain in my heart returned with a vengeance.

Every minute of this day slowed to an agonizing crawl of darkness and desperation.

I yearned for the sun to return and escort in a fresh opportunity to start over. Yet I had a strange feeling the sun would never shine again—at least not as I remembered it.

Although I wanted to make my bench a permanent residence, I knew I had to continue my search for Mama and Mariam. Rubbing my temples, I took a deep breath, and after a moment of deliberation, I stood and looked up. "Help me, God. Please."

Except for periodic flashes of radiant white, the narrow streets were bathed in the dim yellow of flickering torches. The air was oppressive, as if a decaying mantle covered every living thing. But the melancholy mood and intense heat that settled over Jerusalem had little effect on the hectic activities of the marketplace.

The dusty streets and alleyways buzzed like a shaken beehive. Craftsman showcased their works, merchants displayed their wares, herdsman offered their flocks, farmers exhibited their produce, and customers haggled over prices. Accompanied by attendants, citizens of position sorted through the exotic fabrics and inspected the herbs and spices from foreign shores. Slaves selectively chose foods for their masters' tables; pilgrims weaved through the maze of booths and gaily arrayed tables. Peddlers, beggars, and thieves practiced their art on naive pilgrims.

As I maneuvered my way through the mass of people, I examined their faces. Just hours ago, hundreds stood outside the Pavement of Pontius Pilate's court and demanded the death of an innocent man. They watched as he was dragged through the very streets where they now browsed and bargained. They stood by as he was nailed like a piece of butchered meat to a wooden post. Not one had protested.

I felt sick, not by their actions but mine. I also stood outside the Pavement. I watched as he was dragged to that loathsome pile of rock. I stood by as they nailed him to a cross.

But for me, he was no stranger. He was not just another victim of Roman law. He was my mother's eldest son. He was my brother.

I was filled with an intermingling of emotions, from personal loathing to self-pity. I needed to find my mother and ask her forgiveness for not doing something, anything that might have stopped this unimaginable act. I wanted to beg her to absolve me of the guilt of abandoning her and fleeing like a coward. In some feeble way, I wanted to explain my actions, to comfort her, and to be comforted by her.

As I navigated the narrow, dirt-covered thoroughfares, the sound of family revelry resonated off the cobblestone streets. Each house I passed appeared to contain laughing children, loud prayers of thanks, and songs of praise. Such frivolity seemed out of place. Their joy inflicted fresh wounds on my tormented heart.

Knocking on the large wooden door of the home of Moshe and Abigale, old friends and some of those who followed Jesus closely, I announced my presence. Their home was a regular stop when we were in Jerusalem, and Jesus often spoke of the hospitality they had shown him and his followers. Mama and Mariam may have found refuge there.

Impatiently, I pushed the door open and shouted, "Moshe! Abigale! Are you here?" I was answered only by the echo of my own voice. Again I yelled, "Is there anyone here?" And again, silence.

As I stood in the open doorway and gazed down the empty street, listening to the sounds of family gatherings, my attention was drawn to a different sound—more like whimpering. The stone walls, cobblestone street, and noise emanating from neighboring houses made it difficult to identify the source. I entered our friends' home and moved to the center of the room until I heard the sound again. Following the sound, I walked over to a small room that served as a storage and preparation area. The walls were covered with wooden shelves, which held clay pots, bowls, and fabric bundles. In the back corner stood a large chest for clothing and other personal items. Behind the chest, a small cavity in the wall gave access to a narrow stairwell. As I ascended, the whimpering turned to sobs. At the top of the steps, an opening led to the roof where eight adults and three children huddled in a circle. Stepping through the opening, I was greeted by three armed men who stood and surrounded me.

"James!" A friendly voice shouted from those who remained seated. "This is James. He is the brother of our Lord."

The men lowered their weapons to their sides and warm greetings followed. Weeping, Moshe stood and embraced me. As I looked over his shoulder to the others, tears formed in the eyes of both the women and the men.

"James, I am so sorry. We loved your brother. Jesus was our friend, but much, much more. Come, sit with us and eat," Moshe said. "Abigale, get our guest something to eat."

"Thank you, but I cannot stay. I'm looking for my mother and sister. The last place I saw them was where—" I struggled to finish my sentence. Taking a deep breath, I said, "Was where they crucified my brother." The mention of Jesus's death brought more tears from everyone, even the children.

"We saw her there and asked her to come and stay with us. She said she could not leave because she had to complete a task. We offered to help, but she insisted it was something she alone must do," Abigale said.

A mantle of silence settled over us, each contemplating the dreadful events of the day. Only the quiet sobs of broken hearts interrupted the stillness. Abigale took my hand and kissed it as her tears filled my palm.

Moshe placed his hand on my shoulder. "You must be careful, James. The high priest, Caiaphas, has ordered that all the followers of Jesus are to be arrested."

"I'm not a follower. I'm his brother."

"All the more reason you must be vigilant. You will be seen as the next in line to carry on the message," Moshe said.

"Message? What message? All I want to do is find my mother and sister and return to Nazareth."

"Please, my friend, be cautious. Your brother's message of love and peace brought the wrath of Rome upon us, and Caiaphas's jealousy and fear continue to stoke the flames of hatred."

"I will be cautious," I assured them.

Receiving a final embrace from Moshe and Abigale, I thanked them for their hospitality and friendship. Stepping out onto the street and closing the door behind me, I was filled with an overwhelming sense of solitude and separation. Would I find relief anywhere in any measure? My soul felt dead, my mind void of rational thought. A strange sense of comfort fell over me as my hand enfolded the small pouch at my side, which contained a few pieces of my mother's bread. We were never allowed to leave her side without her tender touch upon our cheek and a piece of freshly baked barley bread.

What I once looked upon as an insignificant motherly act now provided the peace I desperately needed. Though filled with sorrow, I was no longer an orphan of affliction.

As the lightning ripped a jagged gash across the blackened sky, my mind traced the image of another, whose peace in a life of pain was acquired just as simply.

◦~∞~◦

Across from the sheep market, outside the gate leading to the Court of the Gentiles, stood the whitewashed terraces of the Pool of Bethesda. Herod built the great structure as yet another monument to his own glory—as if in some way it would buy him peace. As youths, Jesus and I looked forward to returning to Jerusalem to celebrate the Jewish feasts and to see what new edifice Herod Agrippa had erected to himself.

Whenever my brother was in Jerusalem, he visited Bethesda's cool waters. Jesus seemed to take delight in talking to those who gathered there. He said he saw God in the faces of those who craved the pools' comfort and solace. That never made much sense to me, though I met some interesting people the day I joined him.

At any hour, the porches were filled with the weary, ill, and suffering, all seeking asylum from the day's heat or the night's chill. The five verandas facing out in different directions were shaded by hundreds of clay tiles from the banks of the Nile and supported by tall Romanesque columns. The raised wall of the pools sheltered people from the winds. Its stones retained the warmth of the sun, soothing achy or weary limbs. Roman soldiers patrolled the porticos, encouraging the incapacitated and disabled to move on, using the blunt end of their lances as incentive.

Jesus was drawn to the elaborate structure because it had become a haven for the poor, the sick, and the needy. It no longer served only as a place of refreshment for rich travelers. In the splendor of polished marble and crafted slate rested those who could least afford it. "This is what you can expect from God's kingdom, little brother," Jesus said. "Those you least expect will be in residence."

It irritated me when he talked like he had some special insight into God's mind. It made him sound like a know-it-all.

"I don't believe God's kingdom is filled with the sick and crippled," I said. "Besides, these people are here because they can't do anything for themselves."

"You are right on both counts, little brother," Jesus said.

"Stop calling me little!" Straightening my shoulders, I lifted my heels and walked on my toes, hoping to appear older. The effect was short lived. After a few steps, I lost my balance and fell. Heat rose in my cheeks as I picked myself up and followed my brother to the pool.

Maneuvering around deformed, misshapen shells of humanity, we worked our way toward the large pool situated below the terrace. The crystal-clear water reflected the afternoon sun like a massive mirror. The sick and infirmed positioned themselves strategically around the pool so they could view the water without being blinded by the glare of the pool's surface.

I removed my sandals and placed my mantle and belt on a large stone bench. Girding my loins by pulling my tunic up between my legs and tucking it into my girdle, I stepped into the cool waters.

Pointing to a mass of bodies gathered on the deck of the adjoining pool, I said, "Are they not allowed to go into the water?"

"No one wants to disturb the water because many believe that an angel will churn the water in the pool, and the first one to enter the water after that happens will be healed," Jesus said as he joined me.

"Is it true? Does an angel stir the water?" I said, thinking maybe I had just entered a realm where I didn't belong.

"A subterranean stream sometimes bubbles up and disturbs the surface of the pool. That's all," Jesus said.

I felt pity for those broken and weary people. "Why doesn't someone tell them so they don't waste their time waiting here for nothing?" I mumbled. How tragic that they placed their hope in a myth.

I climbed out of the pool and headed for the closest disabled body. With the finesse of a wounded ox, I blurted, "It will do you no good, you know? There are no angels here. You're not going to get any better sitting around expecting something that won't happen."

A man in his late twenties lying on an old dirty cot with withered limbs drawn up under a body covered in rags looked up at me, his face etched with despair. Set deep in his eyes was an understanding of rejection few men would experience. "Does it anger you that we have hope and a place of comfort?" he said.

"You don't understand," I said, bending over to look him in the eye. "I am only trying to help. After you have been here for a while, you will realize nothing is going to happen to heal you."

"I have been here some twenty years. How much longer should I wait to find this out?" He gave me a toothless smile.

"Twenty years!" He had been lying by that pool longer than I had been alive. And for what? "Why do you remain here? Why don't you go to the temple for prayer?"

A flash of anger replaced the sorrowful tone in his voice. "Sit," he said, motioning to a spot next to him.

Looking back over my shoulder at Jesus in the pool, I debated whether to excuse myself and return to the invigorating waters.

"Sit!" he commanded.

Jesus sat by the edge of the pool as I stepped to the man's side and slid down the wall, careful not to jostle his cot or agitate him any further. Stretching out my legs, I accidently pushed the corner of his tunic. Some of the material fell aside and exposed his twisted legs.

"When I was a small boy, I failed to move out of the way of the great Herod's escort and was run over by one of the guard's chariots. There was no money for a physician, so my parents brought me to the temple to be seen by the priest, and as you can see, their pious exercise had little result. I had my day in the courts of God, boy. I have no desire to return to them." He huffed and returned his gaze to the pool, seemingly resigned to a fate that had long since been determined.

"But you have been here for so long waiting for an angel. Why not go to the temple and seek the God who sends the angel?" I was quite proud of the obvious logic in my response. Although the man's voice was laced with venom when he spoke of the temple, Jesus told me later the man's yearslong wait for an angel showed his heart toward God.

Looking at me with eyes that reflected more anger than disappointment, the man said, "The one who represents God in that place told my parents I was not healed because of sin in their lives. If I were to be healed, they needed forgiveness, and that required a sacrifice. Of course, the sacrifice was costly."

"Did they provide the sacrifice?"

"Oh, yes, and many more after that. The priest identi-
fied what was needed each time, and whenever my father
expressed a concern over the expense, the priest said, 'What
is your son worth to you?'" His voice trailed off. "Soon my
parents had nothing left to offer."

"Is that when they began bringing you here?"

"Yes. My mother did. Father left us, and we never saw
him again. I think he felt the sin was his, and it was his fault
I was never healed."

I wanted to tell him of the importance of observing the
traditions of our faith, but the man's bitterness was evident.
His reason for not returning to the temple was obvious, but
I wondered why he continued to come to the pool.

"Does your mother still bring you here each day?"

"No. My mother died long ago. For a while, my brothers
brought me, but soon they tired of the task," he said. "Now, a
few well-meaning people take the time to get me here." Falling back onto his cot, he looked up into the sky and sighed so
deeply I felt sure all breath had been expelled from his chest.

"You are blessed to have such good friends."

Everything went black when my tunic was tossed over
my head.

"Time to go," Jesus said. He then asked the man a question as only he could. "Where is your home?"

If the question had come from anyone else, it would
merely be a friendly inquiry, but Jesus had a way of making you feel your answer could be life changing. Papa often
expressed some concern about the way Jesus asked questions
during study in the synagogue. Although he was respectful

and honored the elders, they told Papa an air of confrontation hung over Jesus whenever he entered the building.

With that same inquiring tone, Jesus posed his question to this poor unfortunate. He wasn't simply asking about a residence; he was seeking the location of the heart.

Hesitating, the man studied my brother's face. "This is my home, and these wretched bodies are my family."

"Would you like my brother and I to move you closer to the pool?" I said.

"I am comfortable here," he said, never taking his eyes off Jesus. "This is my place."

"But you are too far away," I said. "If an angel stirred the pool, you would not be able to enter it from this distance." I didn't understand why he wished to remain so far from his greatest desire.

Placing a firm hand on my shoulder to silence me, Jesus confronted the man again. "Do you know the cost of your healing?"

"I have had much time to consider this," he said. "It is not likely I will sit at the gate with the rich and noble, but here I have my place. This is my gate. I have been here longer than anyone else." With an air of pride, he added, "They call upon me to give counsel."

"Come, little brother. Papa is waiting."

Moved with compassion for the man, I wanted to do something. But what? Leaning over to Jesus, I said, "Shouldn't we offer to help him into the water? At least get him a little closer?"

Dropping his head, Jesus spoke in a low, regretful tone. "For what reason? What he needs will not be found in the water. What he wants, he has already found." Looking directly at the man, he said, "When you are ready, I will return and help you move your cot."

Without another word, Jesus stood and departed through the verandah. Before I followed, I said to my invalid friend, "We'll be back. Keep a close watch on the pool. Your healing will not take too much longer." I only wished to leave him with a glimmer of hope. I do not think I was successful, however, because he looked up at me with a blank stare that told me he no more believed in a future healing than I did.

"I'm sure we will meet again," I said. Reaching into the pouch tied at my side, I removed a piece of Mother's barley bread, bent down, and handed it to him.

"May Jehovah bless you with abundance, my young friend," he said.

From the pool of despair that existed behind his eyes came a glimmer of hope.

⌁∞⌁

To my left came a deep rolling rumble of thunder, awakening me and suppressing the feeling of peace and joy I momentarily had. How could recalling an experience in my youth—a simple, cheap gesture of sharing bread—provide me such comfort? I thought of the gentle hands that made the bread in the pouch at my side and remembered my mother's current anguish.

Setting my past recollections aside, I resumed my search for her by heading toward the Upper City, where other family friends resided. From there, I could move through the marketplace and ultimately to the temple, but my first stop would be the finest potter's house in all Judea.

Sitting among the jars and pots lining the street in front of his home, Azariah deftly formed the neck of a slender water jar on his potter's wheel. "Shalom. Come and sit with me." With a bony, clay-covered finger, he motioned to an open space near the door to his home. "I am sorry to hear of your brother. Hold your anger and remember that God will be your retribution and that Rome will not stand before his wrath."

"Thank you, Azariah. I'm looking for my mother and sister. I last saw them at Golgotha, but I'm sure they left that horrid place."

"You may find them at the home of Moshe and Abigale," he said, without looking up from his work.

"I went there. They were not there."

"Your mother often seeks the company of Mary, John Mark's mother. If she is not at her home or in the Court of Women at the temple, then there is only one other place she would be." His voice trailed off as he looked up but not enough to look me in the eye.

My voice cracked. "Mama may have refused to leave Jesus. She may still be there. She has courage I do not have." I didn't want my voice to betray how I felt, but I lost control anyway. In shame, I dropped my head and cried.

Azariah stood and put his arm around my shoulder. I needed his comfort, but his gesture also compounded my guilt. My mother needed comfort too. No matter the depth of my pain and despair, she had experienced a loss I could not comprehend.

Patting Azariah's hand, I expressed my appreciation and thanked him for his help. The few moments spent with him replenished my spirit. Navigating past the delicate pieces of pottery, I moved toward the temple with newfound virility. My heart remained sad, but I was ready to retake the responsibility of being the eldest son.

Knowing my mother was not alone reassured me. She was with Mariam and most likely with Mary, a woman of substance, both financially and emotionally. She, like Mama, lost her husband early and never remarried, although the Mosaic law permitted it. She had a firm grasp upon the truths of the scriptures, which made me wonder why she became so wrapped up in my brother's teachings. She lent support, food, and shelter to him and his band of spiritual nomads. Her involvement with Jesus had also jeopardized her position within the Jerusalem community.

I heard the Sanhedrin had threatened her with expulsion from the temple if she continued to associate with my brother and his followers. For a woman, even one with financial means, that could have meant death. Yet she continued. Why would a woman risk the comfort of a life her husband worked so hard for—not to mention the security and inheritance of her son—for what I saw as some abstract ideology? It made no sense.

As I navigated the narrow streets of the market, a guttural voice behind me said, "Shalom, peace be with you. Can you help a hungry man on the eve of the Passover?" Turning toward the voice, I was overpowered by the pungent aroma of a man who, no doubt, worked closely with camels and had not bathed in some time.

As he extended an open, dirty hand to me, I noted it was not callused. Aside from the grime, his hands appeared to be those of a merchant or at least someone who had little experience with hard labor.

A sense of indignation welled up within me. "Have you attempted to find work, so you may provide for your own need?"

I assumed my harsh response would put him on the defensive, and he would spew rationalizations of how uncontrollable circumstances and social injustice held him back from his full potential. But to my surprise, his response was anything but excusatory.

"I have been trying, sir," he said. "For the first time in my life, I am trying to provide for myself. I am not trained in any craft, and I know nothing of caring for crop or animal, but I will do anything. Do you have work for me?"

As he stepped closer, I instinctively stepped back. He stood straight, towering over me. His head was topped with a thick mop of unkempt black hair, and his mouth spread into a wide, toothless grin. He was covered in a tattered, brown tunic, which reeked of camel dung. Bathed in the golden hue of torch light, his appearance left me speechless. No wonder he could not find work. I was surprised, however, that even though he had no trade, he appeared to be in good health.

"I have no work for you. I am not from Jerusalem. I am a Nazarene," I said. Why was I wasting my time with this beggar? "Here, take this. It is all I have," I said. Reaching into my pouch, I withdrew a piece of Mama's bread and thrust it into his hands. "I must go."

Holding the fragment close to his chest with both hands, he smiled again. "Thank you. I will one day also know the joy of providing for another, and I will do so in your honor." His face reflected a joy that contradicted his condition. Instead of the lamentable sneer normally painted on the faces of the poor, his face was painted with hope. Watching him walk toward the marketplace, the memory of another acquaintance with a similar expression crossed my mind.

As I continued up the narrow cobbled street, the voice of the beggar echoed off the walls: "May Jehovah bless you with abundance, my young friend."

Those words were familiar; I had heard them before. They were spoken by a man with twisted limbs that served no purpose but to draw the sympathy of strangers. He was a broken man whose life had been spent on a soiled cot, wrapped in rags, waiting upon angels. A man who expressed no hope until my brother assured him that when the man was ready, Jesus would return and help him move his cot.

I watched in awe as he waved and walked away swiftly, disappearing around a corner.

When Jesus saw him lying there and learned that he had been in this condition for a long time, he asked him, "Do you want to get well?" "Sir," the invalid replied, "I have no one to help me into the pool when the water is stirred. While I am trying to get in, someone else goes down ahead of me." Then Jesus said to him, "Get up! Pick up your mat and walk." At once the man was cured; he picked up his mat and walked.

John 5:6–9

CHAPTER SIX
A Prisoner for Life

"Out of the way! Move aside there!"

Before I could respond, the sole of a Roman boot drove into my back with enough force to propel me facedown onto the cobblestone. The clatter of cart wheels generated a fear that inspired me to scramble to the side of the road. I had no desire to see what additional damage a horse's hoof could do to my injuries.

Clearing the road's edge, safe from the crushing hooves and wheels of Roman transportation, I took refuge in a muddy trench. The damp earth of the embankment soaked into my clothing. I sat alone, covered in mud, my body throbbing with pain, heartbroken that my brother was dead, and there was nothing I could have done about it.

Anger welled up within me as a standard-bearing horseman passed by wearing leather boots laced to the knee. Behind him rolled a battle chariot arrayed in multicolored banners. Covered in polished brass, the two-wheeled vehicle reflected the blinding flashes in the afternoon sky. The bright red plume atop the centurion's helmet danced in the breeze as his muscular arms pulled on the reins, restraining the two powerful Arabian steeds. Next to him stood another figure, akin to one of the many Roman statues that had been erected throughout Palestine in honor of some Greek deity. This soldier stood proudly surveying those whom he oppressed. He was not unlike the statues that loomed pompously over those who worshipped them.

The centurion's passenger raised his hand, and the chariot came to an abrupt stop. The company of soldiers that followed closely behind, each clad in full battle armor and toting their weapons, took the opportunity for a small respite, leaning upon lances, shields, and one another.

Turning slightly aside from his comrades, the arrogant representative of Rome's divine elite withdrew a small piece of cloth from under a sash around his waist and covered his nose and mouth, as though the air of Jerusalem was repugnant. He was robed in a pure white toga stitched with gold lace. Draped over his shoulders was a purple cloak with golden tassels at each corner, held securely in place by a dazzling gold-and-silver Roman insignia, which had surely been hand-polished to its present luster.

He carried himself like royalty—the glitter of pendants, rings, and bracelets coupled with aloofness, seemingly oblivious to or at least unmoved by the misery around him. The man, however, did not sit on a throne. He was Romulus Hyrcanus, Pilate's right hand. He represented Rome and stood at my brother's side during the political charade they called a trial. He had read the charges that called for my brother's execution. Anarchy against the state!

Romulus pivoted slowly, pushing aside a large flag bearing the symbol of Rome that obstructed his view. As he looked down at me, covered in mud and sitting in a gully designed to drain sewage, his sneer became mocking laughter. "Look at the little Jew monkey!" he yelled, pointing at me. Turning to the centurion, he said, "See how these wretched people live? Like scum, they make their home in the waste of Rome." With his head held back, he lifted his hands from the chariot's rails, wrapped them around his oversized abdomen, and laughed again.

From deep within me—a deep pit I had never dipped into—came an explosion of irrational rage. Jumping up, I ran toward the chariot. My only desire was to see him draw his last breath. Cresting the edge of the road, I grabbed the leather harness of the closest horse and pulled myself to the side of the chariot. Reaching out, I entwined a slime-stained Jewish hand in the clean white robe of Roman domination. The disruption was more than the Arabian steeds could tolerate. Rearing back, they caused the chariot to heave violently, throwing Romulus and me to the ground. Screaming like a woman in labor, he beat me with two tight fists. "Help! Help! Get this disgusting swine off me!"

I heard a loud crack followed by a shrill howl, like an animal had been wounded. The world shattered into a wide spectrum of reds, blues, and yellows. The vengeance that had seemed so important became grossly inconsequential. As pain coursed through my body, I realized the crack was my skull, and I the creature that howled. A boot struck my abdomen with the force of a boulder—again and again until every part of my body pulsated.

Pushed onto my back, I peered at Romulus through the blood streaked across my eyes.

"Would you have him chained with the others?" said a voice behind him.

"No," Romulus said and leaned over to spit into my face. As he stood, I noted with pride the smeared handprint that soiled his white robe.

Pulling me up into a seated position, the centurion twisted his hand in my hair, withdrew his short sword, and placed it across my throat. "What would you have done with him, your Excellency?"

What a suitable way to end the day. Despite my pain, calmness spread through me. Serenity can accompany apathy, an apathy born out of an indifference to whether I lived or died.

"Nothing!" came the command. "Look at him. Leaving him alive is a fitting punishment. Death would be a reprieve for this mongrel." Placing his foot on my chest, he gave me a sound shove, sending me backward into the sewage.

Why couldn't he have given me death? The verdict he rendered showed a depth of the cruelty I would not have accredited even to him.

Returning to his regal position in the chariot, he signaled for the parade to continue. Watching the procession of armed soldiers, followed by carriages, pushcarts, and wagons laden with the implements of warfare and destruction, I realized for the first time how threatened Rome was of us "Jewish monkeys." During the Passover, Jerusalem swelled with worshippers and pilgrims—tens of thousands. The Romans responded with a noticeable increase of military presence. Troops from throughout Palestine were summoned to make themselves visible and to quell any disturbance. I had never seen so many escort one member of Pilate's court. The Zealots were no doubt creating apprehension and trepidation in their persecutors. The lambs of Judah were striking back.

Close behind the marshaled troops trailed a line of haggard, beaten prisoners, shackled to one another by a thick chain. Without sandals and clothed only in torn, filthy rags, each moved with his head down. Among them were Samaritans, Asians, Egyptians, and Jews. Thieves and murders were bound with those who were but patriots—a demonstration of Rome's contempt for anyone they labeled as anarchists. Whatever their crimes, these prisoners would pay with their lives.

Collapsing against the muddy embankment again, I closed my eyes and waited to die. Death couldn't be far away. Contrary to many people I had known, I had lived a long and good life. Until now, I had stayed out of harm's way.

As another streak of lightning crossed the afternoon sky, interweaving through the dark clouds, I thought of Jesus and his recklessness. I did not make a habit of flirting with death or with those who could inflict it, but that could not be said of my older brother.

⌁⬥⌁

"This will sustain you until you return," Mama said, tucking a tightly wrapped straw bundle into the corner of our pushcart. When she smiled at me, I knew what she had made for our lunch—four cracknels and two pomegranates. Mama knew I loved those hard crumb cakes, and the tasty seeds of the pomegranates were my favorite treat. Slinging a waterskin over my shoulder, Mama handed me another to be given to my brother. With a whisper in my ear, she assured me that a good meal would be waiting for Jesus and me when we got back. After kissing my cheek, she disappeared into the house.

The cart had been loaded with three-legged stools and a variety of short benches. Papa carved the joints and corners to perfection and honed the amber-colored olive wood. Polished to a high luster and fitted with cushions of goatskin filled with loose wool and stitched tightly, each promised the buyer true comfort.

"Seek only grain, oil, or silver in trade," Papa said, tightening the ropes on our cargo. "We need bread, not exotic merchandise. God has provided all we require."

"Yes, Papa," Jesus said as he took a firm hold of the push handles at the rear of the cart. Looping the pull rope that was tied to the front of the cart around my waist, I dug my sandals into the soft clay of the roadway and tugged for all I was worth. With Jesus pushing from the rear, we had it rolling in no time.

Our destination was the intersection of three main caravan routes, just four miles north of our home. Sailing ships filled with goods from throughout the world docked and unloaded their cargo at Ptolemais and Caesarea, where it was packed upon camels and sent throughout Palestine and Syria. The two routes intersected with a third that led to Samaria. The continuous flow of caravans provided a wide variety of potential customers.

The narrow, rough road allowed only a single cart or camel to pass. With their lengthy convoys of beast and men, heavily burdened with exotic items, foreign traders were not about to stop so two Hebrews and a load of stools could cross. So far, we had not encountered any other travelers, which was both good and bad—good because we did not have to maneuver out of their way and bad because many lone travelers along those routes were attacked by thieves.

Coming to the clearing at the summit of a small rise, I saw Sepphoris in the distance. The sunbaked bricks of the caravansary were a welcome sight. There we could rest, eat, and maybe sell some of Papa's furnishings to the road-weary travelers who stopped to take lodging.

From the summit, the road sloped downward toward our destination, making our passage much easier. I shivered in the cool morning dampness as we entered the shadows of a rocky gorge encompassed by tall limestone cliffs. Maneuvering the cart around a slight curve in the road that brought us back into the sunlight, I saw the silhouette of a man, his sword drawn, standing in the road.

"What is in the cart?" he yelled, just as it slammed into the back of my legs and pushed me to the ground.

"Stand up, little brother, and pull," Jesus said, pushing forward.

"There is a man and he has a sword! Can't you see?"

Steadily pushing forward, Jesus barked at me, "Pull, I said. I do not intend to face him in the dark, and I am not leaving the cart behind. Now move!"

Easy for him to say. I was the first who would face that sword, not him.

Moving past our adversary into the sunlight, I felt the cart drag as Jesus stopped pushing. When my eyes adjusted to the light, I realized this man was a boy, but he was not alone. Out of the cave came three more boys dressed in rags, thin and pale but well-armed. Each wielded a staff, sling, or sickle, and their scowls indicated they were willing to use them.

"I asked what you have in the cart," he repeated, and the other boys surrounded us.

"We are taking stools to sell to the caravans," Jesus said with an unusual calm.

"Where are you from?"

"Nazareth."

"Do you have any food?" he said, surveying the contents of the cart.

"No!" I said, almost instinctively.

"Yes," came the voice behind me.

Turning to glare at my brother, I saw that he had already removed the straw bundle and handed it to the leader. Like a pack of wild dogs, the others moved in to get their share.

"Do you have need of water?" Jesus said.

A muffled yes came from the huddle that had formed around my lunch. To my surprise, Jesus removed not one but both waterskins from the cart and handed them to the boys. Without so much as a grunt of appreciation, they retreated back to the caves.

"Let's go!" I shouted. "Before they come back to steal all of Papa's wares."

"They have no need of stools, little brother, but they do need help," he said in a low voice, watching them disappear into darkness. Grasping hold of the push handles, Jesus directed me to guide the cart to the side of the road.

"Why are we stopping? We don't know what harm they may intend for us. We need to get to Sepphoris, where there are civilized people." For the eldest son, Jesus often showed a surprising lack of common sense. Only Jesus would help robbers steal from him and then wait around to see if they wanted more. I loved him, but he bewildered me.

After blocking the wheels with a stone, I stood and found myself alone. Jesus had gone into the cave with them. Had he lost his mind? Looking about, I debated whether I should run to the caravansary for help. But that meant leaving him behind, which I refused to do.

"Come here, little brother." Jesus said from deep within the cave. I made my way toward the sound of my brother's voice, all the while estimating how fast I could run to the caravansary. I bent forward and peered inside. Just inside the mouth of the cave sat Jesus and the pack of thieves warming themselves around a brightly glowing fire.

"Come in and sit with us." Jesus smiled and patted the ground next to him.

In a tone that had lost almost all its fight, I said, "We must get to Sepphoris so we can sell our goods."

"We will not be long," Jesus said in an assuring tone. "Come and sit."

The fire was warm, and it felt good to rest. I hadn't realized how hungry I was until I noticed the crumbs on the thieves' faces and the broken, empty pomegranate shells lying about the floor of the cave.

Uneasiness tumbled in my stomach as the young man who met us at the gorge leaned toward Jesus. His face was hard, and hatred flickered in his eyes. "Let me ask you, Nazarene, do you sympathize with Rome?"

"If you are asking me if I support the Romans, my answer is no," Jesus said.

Sitting back with an air of condescension, the thief said, "We are Zealots. Why don't you join us? Together we will rid our land of these parasites."

"How do you intend to do that? You appear to be only a small band."

"We will meet up with others soon. That's why we are here, to find those who are willing to fight and die for Israel."

I intended to remain silent, but couldn't. "Why do you wish to fight a battle that cannot be won? Zealots have caused disruption since the Maccabees, and it has brought nothing but death and sorrow."

Rage flashed across his face. He turned to me. "What do you know of death and sorrow? You peddle your stools and dine upon crumb cakes. You have come to believe your greatest threat is not Rome but me. You and others like you are apathetic fools. Like you, I once had a brother."

His countenance changed as his anger turned to sadness. "Our mother birthed us on the same day, but Herod, that spineless puppet of Rome, stole my brother from me. We were two years old when Herod's emissaries entered our village, ripped the male children from the arms of their mothers, and slaughtered the boys in the streets. Our mother put rags in our mouths so we could not cry out and hid us under different piles of sheepskins. The soldiers found my brother and assumed they'd found the only male child of the house. I nearly suffocated before my mother retrieved me.

"Was this in Bethlehem?" I blurted.

Nodding, he said, "How do you know this?"

Placing my hand upon Jesus's shoulder, I said, "My brother was born in Bethlehem. If our father and mother had not fled to Egypt, he, too, would have been killed."

An awareness of similar backgrounds gave me ease. I had a common bond with this young man. We shared a common enemy. He and his companions were no longer thieves, and Jesus and I were no longer victims. We were all joint defenders of the right and common casualties of Rome. But my mellow attitude came to a blunt end.

Leaping across the fire pit, the young man pounced on Jesus like a wolf on a lamb. Holding him down by the throat, he demanded, "How was your father warned of Herod's intent? Was he a friend of that pig?"

"No," Jesus said in an unruffled tone that told me who was truly in control. "My father is a friend of God."

The self-proclaimed rebel stared into my brother's eyes with the obvious intent to intimidate. He then moved back to his place and reestablished his position as leader by shoving one of the smaller boys out of his way. "So you believe there is a God, do you?" he mocked.

"The fact that I am here demonstrates that," Jesus said.

"Where was your God when my brother was murdered?"

"The same place he was when you were not." Jesus smiled.

The leader angrily poked at the fire and looked back at me. "The fine families of Bethlehem joined together and demanded we leave the village. I guess they were unhappy I lived."

"Where is your family now?" I said.

"My father was a blacksmith in Gaza, whose craftsmanship was known throughout the region. He forged many Roman weapons with his hands, but his efforts meant nothing to those gluttonous swine. When he stood to defend my mother from the advances of a drunken centurion, he was arrested. Because his back was strong, the Romans sent him to the copper mines in Cyprus, where he was certain to rot and die. Do you still wonder why I am willing to fight to the death?" He snarled at me.

"But what of your mother? If you are dead, who will care for her?"

Hunching over the last bit of cracknel, he gazed into the fire. "To provide food for our family, my mother sold herself. Her best customers were those sanctimonious bloodsuckers who spent their days in the gates of the temple debating the spiritual and their nights indulging in the iniquities available in Jerusalem's alleyways. When she grew old and lost her appeal, she was brought before the very men who knew her best and accused of offending their innocence. When they judged her unfit to live, they made her stoning a public celebration of their holiness."

My heart was so heavy I could not speak. If ever there was a reason to hate, this rebel had one.

With characteristic concern, Jesus said, "Take caution, my friend. The enemy you seek to destroy is not your true adversary. You should prepare for the one who desires to steal your heart before he steals your life."

"That is the difference between me and you, Nazarene. You fight your battles with words. I fight mine with iron." He stood and said, "It is time for you to leave."

Moving toward the mouth of the cave, I reached for one of the goatskins of water. Jesus placed his hand upon mine and motioned for me to leave it.

Outside, our not-so-congenial host had a few more words for us. "Remember, Nazarene, while you and your little brother sleep in the comfort of your home, it is I, and those who follow me, who are willing to give our lives so you may be set free from these Roman leeches."

Removing the shawl from his shoulders, Jesus folded it and handed to him. "A small token of thanks for your sacrifice," he said.

"That's the shawl Mariam made you," I whispered.

"She can make me another," Jesus said. "Give him yours as well."

"What?" They didn't need to steal everything we had. Jesus volunteered it. He not only gave away what had been given to him but also offered what had been given to me. Reluctantly, I removed the shawl from my shoulders and handed it to the boy next to me. Although this displeased me, it was a small price to pay to emerge from the cave unharmed.

"You expect me to thank you for this?"

"No," Jesus said. "You could have taken it. I do have one request, though."

"What is that, Nazarene?"

"Should the day come when someone makes as great a sacrifice for you as you have made for me, I ask that you take a moment and give thanks to God."

Chuckling, he said, "Agreed. But don't expect that to happen within your lifetime, Nazarene."

"I don't, my friend," Jesus said, then took hold of the cart's handles.

⋄∞⋄

The thunder bellowed its deep ovation as I lay coiled like a babe in its mother's womb. I took comfort in the filth and muck that flowed from beneath the city walls. The damp sewage oozed over me, its coolness soothing both my mind and body. How far, I thought, this day has taken me. I awakened with the noble intention of retrieving my brother from the unjust hands of Pilate and ended up in the manure of Rome.

Sensing a presence, I forced open my eyes enough to see a man the size of a mountain standing over me. A flash of lightning illuminated the scarred, distorted features of one who had encountered extraordinary abuse and knew how to inflict such pain upon others. Closing my eyes, I awaited the blows that would surely fall.

A spasm of pain jolted through my gut as two strong hands reached under my arms and lifted me from the sludge that cradled me. Like the carcass of a dead animal, I was tossed onto the hard wooden floor of a small wagon and drifted into unconsciousness.

"Well done, little man." A baritone voice echoed as the world swam back into focus. Pain began to pulse through every fiber of my being. I wanted desperately to return to the painless state of unconsciousness, but that wasn't going to happen.

I opened my eyes and found myself in a large room across from a fireplace casting dancing shadows on the wall. The wall near my cot was lined with shelving; across from me, two open doors led to smaller rooms. To the right of the fireplace, a low-cut wooden door with a cross bar must have opened onto the street.

Rolling onto my back to see the rest of the room, I looked up into the face of pure imperfection. A figure large enough to be a descendant of Goliath towered over me. From his eyes emanated a joy I had encountered in the most unexpected people that day. His feet were bare, and he was dressed in torn sackcloth, similar to that worn by the prisoners I had seen earlier. Had he escaped from those destined for Pilate's prison?

"You were a sight." A soft voice came from somewhere in the room. When I sat up, the room seemed to spin. Placing my fingertips at each temple, I rested my chin in my palms as I looked around. The voice came from a young woman dressed in exotic robes and adorned with anklets, earrings, bracelets, and beads. Her beauty was marred by the garish application of colored pigments and dyes to her face and hands.

In the corner sat two other men. A strange pair. One wore the fine clothing and sandals of a royal official. The other was clothed in the bland, functional attire of a desert nomad.

Sitting on the edge of a padded cot, I realized my soiled clothing had been replaced with a clean robe. My matted hair had been rinsed and my face washed.

The men in the corner did not appear as though they would have taken on the task of my renovation, and the massive hands of the huge man were not able to accomplish the undertaking. Glancing over at the painted lady, I felt humiliated but profoundly grateful. I thought of the care Mama gave me when I had been hurt or sick and suddenly remembered: Mama. I still had not found her. I blurted out, "How long have I been here?"

"Not much more than an hour." My large new friend grinned. "I liked the way you brought Romulus down. Took a great deal of boldness, little man. You are welcome to stay with us as long as you like."

"Thank you, but I am not able to stay. I must find my family. Today my brother was crucified, and my mother and sister are somewhere within the city."

Bending down so he could look me in the eye, he said, "Was he a thief?"

"No," I said. "He has never stolen anything in his life. Pilate feared Caesar and was intimidated by Herod," I said, taking a deep breath to control my anger. "So he killed him." The realization of what I said struck me. I shifted my gaze toward the well-dressed man in the corner. Had my words just become my obituary?

Sensing my concern, the big man said, "Do not worry, my friend. He is a friend too."

"Where am I?" I said.

A dirty, pale blue shawl draped through the handle of a huge clay water pot caught my attention. Along the fringe, the fabric was tied in a series of small, delicate knots. I saw Mariam's fragile hands, diligently working on the finishing touches of a special gift for her big brother.

"Where did you get that?" I pointed at the shawl and leapt to my feet.

"One question at a time, little man. You are at the home of my friend Rachel—just inside the city wall, near the Gate of Ephraim. She tended to your injuries."

"Good. Good. Thank you. But where did you get this?" I repeated, removing the scarf from the pot's handle.

"It was a gift. A boy gave it to me long ago. What is that to you?"

"Was it two boys pushing a cart filled with stools along the route to Sepphoris?"

"Yes," he said, his eyes lighting up. "Are you the Nazarene who gave me the shawl?"

"Yes, I gave you one, but not this one. This was my brother's." My voice quivered and my eyes filled with tears.

"The brother who died on the cross?" he said.

Burying my face within the folds of the shawl, I wept. "Yes."

His voice softened. "I made a promise to the Nazarene. Do you remember? If anyone should do for me something greater than I had done for him, I was to give thanks to God."

Lifting my eyes, I saw a mountain cry. "Yes, I remember."

"Your brother has died so that I might live," he said.

"What?" I was sure the look on my face put emphasis to my question.

His words were garbled as he wept, but I was able to make out one sentence clearly. "I should be on that cross, not him."

That I understood. "I, too, should be on that cross," I said. "I abandoned him and fled when he needed me most."

Handing him the shawl, I shuffled toward the door, then turned. "I must go. Shalom, and thank you for your help."

"You are welcome," he said, clutching the shawl that appeared so small in his massive hands. "I wish I could have thanked your brother, but that is not possible now."

Stepping past me, he opened the door, placed a hand upon my shoulder, and bid me farewell. "If you need anything, just ask for me. Everyone knows who I am."

"Thank you again, my friend," I said, embarking into the darkness. The sky ignited in a blaze as thunder shook the ground.

With his hand raised and a voice deeper than the thunder, he shouted, "Don't forget me, little man. My name is Barabbas."

The chief priests and the elders persuaded the crowd to ask for Barabbas and to have Jesus executed. "Which of the two do you want me to release to you?" asked the governor.

"Barabbas," they answered.

Matthew 27:20–21

CHAPTER SEVEN

The Heart of God

With every step I took, my battered muscles cried out for relief. The heat had subsided, and breathing became less labored. Continual eruptions of lightning across the afternoon sky provided the occasional opportunity to get a proper heading and set my course.

The fresh clothing and brief rest revitalized my spirit and provided the strength needed to continue my quest. My pace slowed, but my determination intensified. Limping through the darkness, I weighed the various possibilities of where I might find my family. Although I knew Mama and Mariam were probably at the foot of my brother's cross, I chose to consider every other place first. I had no desire to return there.

Setting out in the opposite direction of that abominable hill, I moved as fast as my wobbly legs could carry me. Lumbering onto the main street heading south, I walked in streets abandoned by the rush of city dwellers and village migrants. Pilgrims and residents alike had sought shelter from the storm and a place to partake in the Passover Seder. Working my way through the Tyropoeon Valley, I caught sight of the Citadel's lofty towers. Phasael, Hippicus, and Mariamne had built them along the wall at the Jaffa Gate in a vain attempt to repel the onslaught of foreign invaders.

What foolishness! While Jews in Jerusalem celebrated their ancient exodus to independence, these Roman spires of self-defiance acted as lookouts to flush out any perceived Jewish zealot.

Adjoining the Citadel, among the mansions and auspicious abodes of the wealthy, stood Herod's palace. Ominous dark clouds laced with erratic bursts of light hovered over its massive limestone walls. The burnished domes and finely cut marble bounced each flash back into the darkness like an arrow off a polished shield. The gloom of the afternoon sky absorbed each reflection as though it had fallen into dyed wool. Venders desperate for that last sale of the day hawked their wares from booths along the base of the palace wall.

An outburst of laughter drew my attention to a stream of yellow light flowing from an open doorway. The limp and apparently lifeless body of a Roman soldier rolled into the street followed by two staggering but upright shadows. Giggling like children, the men lifted their inebriated comrade and struggled to maintain balance. The heavy wooden door of the inn slammed shut with a resounding farewell.

As the weaving trio stumbled toward me, I searched for an escape route. I did not want a confrontation with these drunken bullies. Stepping into the shadows of a doorway, I pressed myself into the corner between the wall and the door with such force I thought I would melt into the mortar. As they approached the alcove where I hid, their slurred babble sounded more like human speech.

"Give me that thing! He has no need of it," barked a deep, raspy voice.

The response was quick and curt. "He won it fairly, but you're right, he has no use of it, but then neither do you!" The voice morphed into a low growl. "If anyone deserves the spoils, it's me."

As the three dimly lit outlines came into view, I realized that, if I could see them, they could see me. Taking a deep breath, I pressed deeper into the shadows. Stopping within arm's reach of my asylum, the two soldiers loosened their grip upon their flaccid companion, and gravity took control.

A sympathetic pain shot through my stomach as I watched him fall facedown onto the cobblestone pavement with a sickening, dull thud. His comrades then turned their attention to an object wrapped around his prone, slumped shoulders. Simultaneously, each bent over and took hold of a large piece of woven cloth. They pushed, pulled, and snapped at each other like a couple of wild dogs.

Creeping toward the shadow's edge, my heart pounded so loudly I feared it would draw their attention. Readying weary limbs to make a run for it, I looked one last time toward what had become a brawl.

Edging forward, my eyes beheld something frighteningly familiar. A series of small, delicate knots were tied along the hem of what was quickly becoming a rag in the hands of those brutes. Could nothing be kept from such jackals? The few remaining possessions of a dead Jew had become the object of a drunken squabble. Another battle began, but this time it raged within me. *Do I reach out and retrieve the last remnant of what was my eldest brother's only possession from the grasp of these drunkards, or do I use the drunken fray as an opportunity for escape?*

The debate was quickly settled as the door opened behind me and a hand took hold of my shoulder, yanking me inside. A hooded figure closed the door and latched it. I had been drawn into a large courtyard. Around the perimeter, a number of flickering oil lamps and small but well-managed fires burned. Each fire served a cluster of three to five people. Wide-eyed, they stared at me with misgiving as they huddled under a straw canopy that extended out from the walls.

"Welcome," a deep voice said from the far side of the court. "If you come in peace, you are welcome here."

I smiled, extended my arms out, and opened my hands so they could see that I wasn't armed. Soon, all eyes had returned to their respective fires, and the hooded figure had taken a seat at a small table in the corner.

Stepping back toward the door, I moved along the wall and found a crack in the shutters of a window large enough to peer through. Watching as the drunken trio of Rome's finest staggered out of sight, I strained to see what they had done with my brother's robe. Staring as intently as I could, the dark street burst into brilliant light as a flash of lightning burst across the cobblestone alley. Pushing away from the window, the intensity of the flash caused pain to shoot through my skull like a hot poker.

Covering my eyes in the sleeve of my tunic, I stood motionless for a long moment. When I opened my eyes again and looked toward the street, I saw nothing but shadows. Had I been struck blind? Had I lost not only my brother but also my sight? A hand clasped mine and led me across the courtyard to a secluded corner. By the size of the hand and tenderness of the touch, I knew a woman guided me.

"Sit here," she said. Pressing my back against the wall, I slid down and drew my knees tight against my chest.

"Stay here; I will be back."

Within a few moments, she returned and covered my forehead and eyes with a cool cloth. "Hold this," she said, lifting my hands to the damp fabric. "Sit here for a while; you'll be safe."

"I'm blind," I said.

Patting my hand she said, "My brother was too close when the lightning struck. His hands were burned and he lost his sight, but he healed, and his sight returned as will yours in due time. Now rest, and I will get you some food."

Her footsteps faded. Engulfed in darkness and feeling helpless, I listened to the sounds of strangers milling around and wondered what else this day could possibly have in store for me. Laying my head against the wall, I groaned a prayer—a deep, desperate prayer. "Lord, please, please give me peace. Show me where I must go, what I must do. O Lord, comfort this wretched . . ." The words caught in my throat. With all those who truly needed God's intervention on this horrid day, how could I send such a whimpering, selfish prayer heavenward?

In spite of my self-loathing, a peace settled over me. I took in the familiar aroma of maror, haroset, and roasting lamb. The maror, or bitter herbs, always made my nose and eyes run. But the bitterness made everything else taste sweeter. Papa said maror helped God's people recall how bitter life had been for their ancestors as slaves. Maybe I needed to remember that life was never intended to be heaven on earth. Why would anyone seek heaven if it were?

As children, my siblings and I always looked forward to the presentation of the haroset. The opposite of the maror, haroset was so sweet that after one taste everything else seemed more bitter. Papa said haroset reminded us of the sweetness of the promised messiah's love and freedom.

Outside, the darkened sky exploded into another angry blaze of light. My mind wandered to a much better time.

⌒≫⌒

One dark, cool morning, Mama's voice was soft but firm as she leaned over me. "Up, up my little pup. We must be on our way," she whispered and kissed my forehead. Returning to the fire in the center of our camp, she continued to prepare the morning meal.

Rolling onto my back, I looked out from under my blanket as the initial rays of the sun peeked over the horizon. The autumn foliage along Israel's pathways presented a spectacular display of colors. Leaves of bronze, green, gold, and purple turned a monotone landscape into a beautiful tapestry. Rising up along the outer edge of our encampment was the tall squill plant, whose vivid blue, white, pink, and purple blooms welcomed the seasonal transition.

We had joined three other families and a caravan of merchants traveling south. Large groups were less likely to be robbed along the way. Papa was confident we would find similar companions on our return trip. Our camp was a series of tents and bedding placed in a large circle. The donkeys, goats, camels, and sheep, along with parcels and bales of merchandise, were placed in the center of the circle for safekeeping. We usually stopped and spent the night outside a village or town where we could purchase necessities and the merchants could sell their wares. Mama and my sisters slept in the tent; Papa, my brothers, and I slept outside.

Lying still, I watched a nest of wagtails perform their unique dance, wagging their tails feverishly and prancing around a cluster of speckled eggs. The weather had become unpredictable—one day as warm as summer and the next rainy and cold. The energetic, colorful birds with their perpetual motion signaled the coming of winter.

On the second day of our journey to Shechem, we joined other family members before the winter rains made it too difficult to travel. Shechem was a midpoint for most of Papa's family, so most only traveled two to three days. Papa wanted to ensure that we met all our extended family, and this year he felt the time was right. Most of the children were older and stronger, able to travel without the attention and care necessary when they were younger. Because they no longer need to be carried, they could walk alongside the older family members and participate in the setup and teardown of our camps.

As the wagtails entertained me and the sun greeted the day, the aroma of warm bread danced under my nose. Giggles of childish mirth provided a happy tune in the brisk morning air. Our caravan of travelers had been awake for some time preparing for the day's journey—all except one. Me. Wrapped snuggly in my cover, I hoped Papa thought it more expedient to put me in the cart, as I had been for the balance of the journey. My fanciful musings ended abruptly when someone bounced me firmly but lovingly out onto the ground.

Papa stood above me with my blanket in hand and a broad grin. "Go help your mother."

Coming up quietly, I touched Mama's shoulder, kissed her cheek, and snatched a piece of warm bread from the fire. With a playful slap on the wrist, she shooed me away, but not before I noticed the open spaces between the pieces of bread—telltale signs that other hands had grabbed some of Mama's culinary efforts that morning.

"Find your brother. It's time to eat," Mama said.

"Which one?" I said with a smirk.

Mama, with an understanding twinkle in her eye, turned and looked at me over her shoulder. I knew which brother needed to be fetched—the incessant wanderer.

Tossing the warm bread from hand to hand, I surveyed the landscape. Before me was movement like the ebb and flow of a living wave. The haven at Sychar was the best known and most extensively used traveler's retreat along the route from Galilee to Jerusalem. Although it wove its way through Samaria, it afforded the rest that safety in numbers brought as well as fresh water and the ability to purchase wares from traveling merchants. At Sychar, Isaac's son Jacob, whom God renamed Israel, purchased land and dug his well.

During past journeys to Jerusalem and Bethlehem, Papa told us Jacob's stories as we sat around the campfires. He passed a small jar of water for each of us to drink from and told us that the water came from the very well Jacob had dug so long ago. Because the well did not draw from a standing aquifer but from a flowing underground stream, it was called living waters. All of us sat in wide-eyed silence as Papa recounted the exploits of the Hebrew patriarchs and matriarchs.

The bread cooled, and I savored every morsel as I strolled through the encampments of nomads, immigrants, refugees, and pilgrims. Long ago, I had concluded that looking for my elder brother was the prime reason God placed me in the family of Joseph. Jesus always wandered off, making conversation with anyone willing to exchange ideas. But finding him was never easy. With his wanderlust, he could be anywhere.

Maneuvering around the huddles of humanity, careful not to bump into anyone or disturb their animals, I searched for any group that appeared to be in deep discussion. But Jesus was nowhere to be found.

When I reached the outer threshold of the encampment, I walked with caution along the edge where the outcasts, exiles, and those stricken with various maladies set their tents. They were not allowed to move any closer to the general population, nor were they permitted to use the communal fires or drink from the well. I learned two lessons long ago—the first, not to get too close to them, and the second, Jesus would probably be among those unfortunate outcasts.

I found him nearby, standing motionless near a gnarled old fig tree and staring intently at a lone figure shrouded in a faded veil. I stepped to his side, but before I could speak, he gestured for me to be silent.

"It's time to eat," I whispered. I reached for his arm, but he pulled away and put his arm around my shoulder.

Leaning to my ear, he said, "Watch."

Within a few moments, another person appeared—a tall, bearded man clothed in dark robes. He carried a large bundle of what appeared to be rags. Stopping just short of the lone seated figure, he tossed his load to the ground. The figure on the ground looked up and the veil fell away, revealing a young woman whose dirty face was marbled by tears. The bruising on her face was evident even from a distance. Her eyes and lips were swollen with a deep, though partially healed, cut above one eye.

Neither spoke, but they communicated as distinctly as if they were shouting at one another. Her face registered fear, and her eyes pleaded for something she seemed to know would be withheld—reconciliation. The young man's countenance conveyed indifference, and his eyes held no compassion.

Reaching out, she grasped the hem of his garment and attempted to pull him closer. Studying his face and apparently finding not even the slightest glimmer of compassion or feeling, she wept. He wrenched himself free from her grasp and withdrew a few coins from a pouch. He tossed them onto the rags and walked away, never looking back.

She fell onto the heap of fabric, sobbing. Jesus took a few steps forward, stopped a reasonable distance away, and spoke softly. "Do not despair."

His words carried a level of authority and assurance that seemed to calm her, although her face remained buried in the rags.

"What are you doing?" I said as loudly as I dared. "She's a Samaritan, and this is none of our concern!"

"How can you say that, little brother? Isn't everyone's pain the concern of someone?"

"Maybe so, but this one isn't ours!"

The woman lifted her head and turned her gaze toward us. Wiping the tears from her eyes, her expression hardened. "What do you know about despair?" She almost spat out the words. "Leave me alone. The young one has spoken truth. It's none of your concern." Standing up, she picked feverishly through the rags, retrieved the coins, and thrust them into the pocket of her robe.

"Love is not found in the embrace of men but in the heart of God," Jesus said, with an all-too-familiar tenderness.

I couldn't believe my ears. Grabbing his arm, I said, "What? What?" He was talking to a woman about love, and a Samaritan woman at that. He had lost his mind. "We have to go now!" I shouted.

"In a moment," he said.

She turned to me and scowled. "What do you know about love or about anything that happens between a man and a woman? You're a child. Go away!" She snarled, gathering what was left of her earthly belongings.

"I know God's love for you is greater than any man can give, and he will always be with you." Jesus picked up two pieces from the pile and handed them to her. "He will never abandon you or harm you." Lowering his voice so I could barely hear, he added, "Or divorce you."

That struck a nerve. Dropping the rags, the woman took one step toward us, and the mixture of anger and anguish in her eyes prompted me to step back and almost stumble. Lifting a tattered piece of parchment into the air she shouted, "This is all that love promises . . . a life filled with pain and heartache!" She paused and her voice trailed off. "And now . . . divorce." Glaring at me and then at Jesus, her eyes filled with rage and undisputed resignation. She said, "Go home. Go back to your happy family. You don't belong here." She bent down to gather the pieces of fabric.

Her rage startled me. Although a petite woman, such unrestrained anger could result in grievous consequences. What might she do if Jesus didn't stop talking? I tugged on his arm, but he remained immovable. He then did what I feared he would do.

He spoke to her again.

"The psalmist says that the Lord will watch over the foreigner, and he will care for the fatherless and the widow," he said.

"I'm not a foreigner. You are. And I'm not a widow!"

"We are all foreigners," Jesus said, "and you are as surely widowed as any woman whose spouse has died."

Pivoting to fix her gaze on Jesus, she stood motionless for a long moment, looking into his eyes. "I will accept God's provision and care, but in the meantime I must eat. If someone is willing to provide for me, be it God or someone else, I will welcome the kindness with gratitude. Now go away." Lifting her bundle onto her head, she walked away, her gait slightly bent.

Even though I was a child, I did not think the weight of her load caused the unnatural bend. It was the weight of sorrow and disappointment. I tightened my grip on Jesus's arm, concerned he might follow her. He did not move until she had disappeared into the crowd of sojourners.

"Let's go. The food is cold now, and Papa needs help," I said, tugging on his arm again. "And let's not tell anyone about this. They wouldn't understand. I certainly don't."

Walking back, I noticed a Roman bivouac set up on the far side of the encampment. "Look!" I said, pointing to a centurion standing guard by a large tent.

Jesus stared beyond my extended finger. With a strange sadness in his voice, he said, "So much sorrow, so much pain before peace will ever be realized."

"I know," I said. "Papa says that there will be much hardship before Rome leaves Palestine."

"Rome inflicts adversity upon the nation, little brother, but it can never inflict as much misery as we choose to place upon ourselves," he said, looking down as we maneuvered our way back along the path. "Peace can be ours, but we must choose to accept it."

An explosion of thunder shook the courtyard so violently that dust and mortar fell from the walls. A woman screamed and children cried. There were no fires or torches, and with the shutters closed, I felt uncomfortable in that dismal place. I searched the open area but could only discern shadowy outlines of people clustering together along the court's perimeter. Their dark shapes indicated my vision was improving, but I wondered if I would ever see clearly again.

Placing my hands at my sides to shift my weight, I hit something near my leg that made a clinking sound.

"That's water and food," said a man's raspy voice off to my right. "The woman brought it for you."

Reaching out somewhat warily, I took hold of a small jug and raised it to my lips. I let the cool water run down my throat and over my face and chin. Wetting my sleeve, I rubbed my eyes.

"Where is she?" I said. "The woman. Is she here?"

"She has gone to be with the Master."

I tried to piece together where I was and who these shadows in the dark might be. Were they the disciples of one of the Pharisees or Sadducees who came to Jerusalem to celebrate the Passover? Were they families like my own, too small in number to completely consume the Paschal Lamb and thus required to eat in a group setting? If so, then who was "the Master"?

All sorts of scenarios flooded my mind. Had I been saved from those drunken bullies by a house full of slaves? Whatever the case, these people seemed warm and caring—a contrast to what most likely awaited me outside these walls.

Gradually my sight cleared, and I could make out who were the children and who were the adults. A short distance to my right sat a man near the wall eating from a wooden bowl. Assuming he was the one who had spoken to me earlier, I said, "My name is James. I'm from Nazareth."

He lifted his face from the bowl, stopped eating, and stared at me. As my eyes focused, I noticed that most of the other adults also watched me. A hush fell over the group, the only sound coming from squirming babies cradled in their mothers' arms.

Now that my vision had improved, I realized my companions were all Samaritans. "Who brought me in?"

"The woman," said a man on my left.

"What is her name? I would like to thank her."

"Her name is Photine," the man responded with a trace of irritation. "And as I said, she is with the Master."

"Who is the Master?" I said, and even the babies seemed to go silent.

The answer came from several at once. "You do not know?"

To my right, a large man resting against the wall slowly rose to his feet and stepped toward me. "You are from Nazareth, and you do not know the Master?" he grumbled. "How are your eyes? Can you see more clearly yet?"

"Yes. They are better."

"Good." He reached down, took hold of my arm, and helped me to my feet. "Time for you to go."

"I want to thank Photine for her kindness."

"She is with the Master, and we have come here to be with him too." Reaching behind him, he retrieved a small piece of cloth and placed it in my hand. "Photine said I should give this to you."

I saw a torn piece of tightly woven cloth—a little larger than my hand with a series of small, delicately tied knots along the hem. It was from the robe Mariam had made for Jesus, the same robe those drunkards had torn to pieces as they brawled in the street.

A small boy opened the front door as the man ushered me out. "Be safe," he said, then stepped back into the courtyard and closed the door behind him. I stood alone in the street.

I held in my hand the precious remnant of a garment my elder brother treasured. Stuffing the cloth into my pouch, I looked up and down the street trying to get my bearings and again set out to find my family. Just as I was about to turn a corner, a door opened behind me.

"Wait! I almost forgot," shouted the man from the courtyard. "Photine wanted me to tell you the cloth is from the Master's robe." Scratching his head, he added, "She wanted me to make sure I said this next part right." With a broad smile, he met my gaze. "Do not despair. Love is not found in the embrace of men but in the heart of God." Then he turned and walked away, obviously pleased that he had delivered Photine's message accurately.

I thought back to another encounter with a petite broken woman who, like myself, faced an uncertain future. Reaching into my pouch, I retrieved the small, torn fragment and held it in my palms for what seemed like an eternity. I stroked the coarse weave and rolled the small bows back and forth between my fingers. Each time my fingers caressed the delicate knots, another treasured and precious memory of joyous days spent with my elder brother flashed through my mind. This tattered remnant had become my most prized possession.

My reverie was interrupted when a streak of lightning crossed the darkened sky and illuminated the street like midday. A low contemplative voice whispered softly—a familiar voice because it was my own—"from the Master's robe."

Was that a question or a declaration?

He told her, "Go, call your husband and come back." "I have no husband," she replied. Jesus said to her, "You are right when you say you have no husband. The fact is, you have had five husbands, and the man you now have is not your husband. What you have just said is quite true." . . . The woman said, "I know that Messiah" (called Christ) "is coming. When he comes, he will explain everything to us." Then Jesus declared, "I, the one speaking to you—I am he."

John 4:16–18, 25–26

CHAPTER EIGHT
Most Precious Gift

Standing motionless in the center of the flagstone walkway that led through the northern wall into the Upper City, I looked up and down the wide, fashionable avenues. Here, the wealthy huddled comfortably, finding refuge from the working class. Along the cleanly swept pavement stood the whitewashed abodes of powerful Jewish families and high-ranking Roman officials. In front of Herod's palace, distillers of quality oils, weavers of fine silks and cloth, goldsmiths and silversmiths, and sellers of quality goods set up their booths in the open courtyard.

Today, however, although the tents and shelters of the merchants had been erected, the merchants and craftsmen were nowhere to be seen. The Sabbath began in a few hours, and all work had ceased.

I turned onto a quiet avenue cluttered with empty booths, tables, and bins. Papa came here to sell assorted handmade items when work was slow at home. This portion of the market traded in good but less valued merchandise. It was close to the homes of the affluent but not visible from them.

When I had walked midway down the street, the sound of horse's hooves clattered behind me. Stepping to the side between several empty tables, a small band of mounted Roman soldiers paraded by.

The last in line slowed. "Stay off the streets," he growled. "We're moving supplies and equipment. Go inside where it's safe."

How bizarre. Those who had little regard for our lives, our traditions, or our land spoke of our safety. Safe from what? Safe from them?

Horse-drawn carts came up from behind the mounted soldiers, passed them, and disappeared into the darkness of the Lower City.

Backing up against the wall, I searched the empty street for a doorway, alleyway, or crevice I could take refuge in. My peripheral vision caught a slight movement to my right.

Focusing on a group of tables resting up against the wall surrounding Herod's palace, I watched for activity. None. Turning back, I saw the lead horsemen clearing the corner. From behind him came a loud rumble.

The Romans always took good advantage of Sabbath rest. Unfortunately, the streets would not remain quiet long. I had witnessed Romans move men and equipment from one place to another. They considered nothing other than reaching their goal. Those in command received incentives of gold and rank for swift transport. If that meant running over someone, then so be it. Only the welfare of Rome and those who serve it mattered.

Pressed against the wall, I watched a mounted centurion enter the end of the avenue followed by two standard bearers. One man carried the *imago* that displayed the image of the emperor; the other held the *vexillum*, a deep red banner indicating that the preceding horseman was a high-ranking cavalry officer called a *praefectus alae*.

His glare made me feel as if I were encroaching on his domain. "Stay out of the way," he barked.

I moved as close to the wall as possible. Two horse-drawn carts filled with bundles reached the corner to my left and proceeded down the street, fading out of sight behind the standard bearers.

The rhythmic cadence of soldiers marching in unison grew louder. A recurrent drumbeat in the background set the pace. Entering the avenue, they marched three abreast. The clouds danced like a candlelit tent in the wind as the lightning cast a surreal halo over the helmet plumes of those in the lead.

A company of about eighty soldiers trudged past. Although their cadence was in tempo, the day's journey had taken its toll. When they approached the wall around Herod's palace, a centurion shouted a command that seemed to revitalize them. Backs straightened, heads lifted, and the drumbeat quickened. They marched with an arrogance undoubtedly intended to demonstrate their dominance over Jewish leadership.

Some distance behind the soldiers rode a single horseman leading twenty men wearing loincloths. They were spaced several paces apart, a rope belt around each waist loosely tethered to the horseman in the lead.

While traveling to Jerusalem, we encountered a group like this one. Papa said that the men had been soldiers but were now prisoners working off some penance.

As they walked, they cleared the path by picking up, throwing, or pushing anything in the way. They tossed tables, benches, and equipment against the walls.

Riding behind the men in loincloths were two mounted centurions—one held a staff, the other a whip. As they passed, the prisoners gave me the same hateful glare I received from the soldiers. While the procession worked its way down the street, I caught sight of the elusive movement I had seen earlier by the palace wall.

My attention was drawn to the end of the street by a sound as loud as thunder, which caused the ground to shake beneath me. I did not know what approached, but it had to be large.

A man of sizable girth led four massive oxen that pulled an enormous wagon overflowing with an assortment of armaments and provisions. The narrow thoroughfare could not accommodate the wagon, but the large man leading it was undeterred. Turning the corner, the wagon caught the wooden poles that supported a thatched cover over a merchant's booth, tearing it down along with several others and trampling everything under its wheels.

No sooner had this behemoth moved a short distance down the street than another appeared, and then another. Of similar size, each left mere thumb-breadths between the massive wheels and the wall. To avoid being crushed, I had to find a different refuge.

Getting in front of the first wagon, I climbed over strewn benches, broken tables, and debris, then ran down the street. I saw movement beneath a table that had not been upended. Bending down to rescue what I assumed was an animal from its potential doom, I looked into the fear-filled eyes of a girl of about twelve.

Reaching for her arm, I said, "Come."

She pulled back and shrieked.

"I'm not going to hurt you. We must get away from here. Come."

I looked over my shoulder. No escape. I grabbed the edge of the table. Lifting it onto its edge and grabbing the girl with my other hand, I tugged her to her feet. Pushing her into a recess in the wall that had once been a door, I pulled the table behind me. I put my back against the girl, pinning her into the nook, and positioned the table between me and the oncoming wagon.

Closing my eyes, I held the table in place with all my strength as the wagons passed, their wheel hubs scraping its wooden surface. As the first wagon passed, I took a deep breath, but within moments another emerged, chipping and tearing away pieces of the table. With a sudden yank, what remained of the table was wrenched from my grasp. Supports for field artillery protruded over the sides of the last wagon. Turning, I nestled the girl against my side. Sheltering her as best I could, I pressed into the recess.

Pain shot through me as the end of a support pole for a ballista catapult pierced my tunic and dug into my back. Catching the fabric, it dragged me along like a child's puppet. Releasing the girl, I shouted, "Run! Run!" Instead, she slid down and wrapped her arms around her legs, watching me disappear with a look of stark terror.

Suspended by the support pole, my feet dragged along the cobblestone as I backstepped as fast as I could, trying to get upright. In front of me, a small troop of low-ranking soldiers marched behind the cart. Watching me try to free myself, they pointed, laughed, and joked about the little Hebrew puppet.

Grasping the pole and pulling the fabric with my last ounce of strength, I ripped my tunic free. Attempting to get my feet underneath me, I lost balance and fell hard onto the pavement. Rolling to the side of the road, I barely avoided being trampled under Roman boots.

Lying in the gutter, I looked heavenward and watched as the clouds continued their rhythmic, radiant dance. A streak of lightning formed a bony hand, its finger pointing back to where I had come from. Was it a divine reminder that something, or someone, needed my attention?

Staggering to my feet, I moved slowly but deliberately back along Herod's wall. I found the pile of splintered wood from the table but no girl.

"Little girl!" I shouted. I scanned the devastated market and called, "Where are you?"

An eerie silence followed. Even the lighting that rolled through the clouds made no sound. Sitting where she had once been, I focused on the darkened sky but could barely discern the outline of the clouds as they drifted across the heavens. They looked like the dyed cotton Mama used as she wove fabric in the cool of the eve. I closed my eyes and let my mind drift.

◦⟨∞⟩◦

Standing in the doorway of our home, I saw Mama and Papa together again. Their love was always evident by the words they shared and the way they looked at each other. When Papa would walk past her as she worked at the loom, he would touch her hair and catch her eye. She would bring Papa water in his shop, compliment his skill, and kiss his cheek when she left.

But this time it was different. The love was there, maybe even more now than ever, but this wasn't the same. Mama stroked his hair, gazing at him with a love that only time could build. Caressing his cheek, she leaned over and brushed her lips against it, then spoke words so quietly they were indiscernible to the rest of us. Stepping back, she said, "I love you."

In the corner of the room, my brother sat on a tall stool, raising a finger to his lips. I remained quiet. Mama held Papa's hand as her shoulders shook and tears fell. Her voice trembled when she glanced our way and said, "Jesus, James, get your brothers and sisters. We must prepare your father."

Earlier that morning, Jesus and I had retrieved several planks for Papa to make a grain box for one of our neighbors. When we brought them into his work area, he was leaning over a table with his face in his hands.

"Clear that bench," Jesus said, stepping behind him. Putting his arms under Papa's, he lifted him and guided him to the bench. "Go get Mama," Jesus said. I had seen Papa in pain before—a slip of a hammer, his back out of place, a fall—but the tone in Jesus's voice made my heart skip a beat. This was serious.

Mama entered. She told me to wait outside and keep my younger siblings from coming in. After some time had passed, I heard a low, mournful cry, like the sound a lamb makes when sacrificed on Passover. Mama was weeping. Jesus came out and said with a resignation in his voice I had never heard, "Papa has gone to be with his father. He is with God."

I stood silent, not knowing what to say or do.

Jesus said, "James, come." Going into the work area, he said, "Help me." Together we moved Papa into the house and laid him on the bed while Mama gathered our siblings around it.

Tears flowed like rain as we stood motionless, watching Mama love her husband who was no longer present. Jesus walked over to me, put his hand on my shoulder, and whispered, "Come, we have work to do. Let's leave them alone." Outside, he wrapped his arm around my shoulder and drew me close. I leaned my head against his and we wept.

"Time to help Mama," Mariam said. Although she spoke tenderly, we understood she had given a directive, not a suggestion.

"You are right, little sister," Jesus said as he wiped his face dry. "Take the young ones to the home of Josiah and Rebecca and tell our cousins of Papa's passing. Ask them to watch the children, then get the shroud and sudarium that Mama keeps in her cabinet."

Turning to the rest of us, he said, "Joses, see if you can find myrrh and aloes. If we have none, go to our neighbors. James, fill two large water jugs and bring them to Mama. Then seek out as many of our family as you can and share the news of Papa's death. Return quickly. We need you."

Reaching down and picking up Judas and Rachel, Jesus said, "God, our Father in heaven, has blessed us with a wonderful mother and father who have shown us how to live and how to love. They have loved and served God our Father with their words, their lives, and their hearts. Papa has taught us that God has appointed a time when He will call each of us to our home in heaven. This is the time God has chosen for his servant Joseph to come home."

"Why now?" cried Rachel.

"It is not for us to question God's plan but to accept His love and trust Him," Jesus said as Rachel snuggled closer and laid her head on his shoulder. "Our heavenly Father showed His compassion by giving us life and assuring that we were mature enough to be at Mama's side to help her in this sorrow. Let us each do what we can to lighten Mama's burden. Now, do as I have told you," he said. "I will go to the synagogue and talk to the rabbi."

When I returned, Jesus and Joses were sitting in the courtyard with a boy a little older than myself. He wore a *sādhīn* of fine linen under his tunic. At each corner of his cloak, a *tzitzit* was sown—a small tassel that reminded him to keep the commandments of the Lord. On his head, he proudly wore a *kaffiyeh* with a colorful band.

Looking up, my brother waved me over. "James, this is Jairus. He has come with his father from the synagogue. The rabbi is with Mama and Mariam. They will call us when they are ready." Taking my seat, I noted the boy wore a gold ring engraved with a menorah.

A long silence fell over the courtyard as we pondered the day's events. That morning, we had stood together and prayed, giving thanks for the day, for our family, our home, and our food. I felt ashamed because my mind had wandered, as it often did, far from our morning prayers to adventures I had planned.

We ate with Papa as he instructed us in being thankful when things were good and even more grateful when they were not. That morning Papa had pointed to Simon, who recently celebrated his birthday, and asked him to lead us in prayer. Papa said he was ready to take a greater part in the family worship.

Taking a deep breath, Simon began by giving thanks, first for his sandals, then for his clothes, and finally for his toys.

Mama said, "What about your brothers and sisters?"

"Oh, and them too," he said, stepping back and stretching as tall as any five-year-old could. He looked around at each of us, and we gave him an approving nod and smile. His chest puffed out and a broad grin covered his face.

Papa had also assigned each of us tasks for the day. I was to clean his work area and help deliver a grain box he was working on and would have completed by midday. But that would not happen today; neither would any of our other plans be fulfilled. Papa was no longer here. Tears returned to my eyes, and Jesus moved closer so I could bury my face in his shoulder.

"I'm sorry for your loss," Jairus said. "Do you believe in the resurrection? I attend the Bet Midrash and study the Halachot along with the writings of the Prophets. There is a grand library there, and I have read much from the great teachers about when the soul is reunited with the body."

He probably intended for his words to bring hope into our despair, but my mind was not on what may happen someday. I had lost my father, and my thoughts centered on what had happened today.

When none of us responded, Jairus said, "I want to believe that, but I don't. How is it possible for the dead to live again?"

My heart sank a little bit further.

Jesus said, "Nothing is impossible for God. The power of life is in His hands, my friend. One day you will know that power."

"Brothers, bring the children and come," Mariam said, holding open the door.

The room was filled with the smell of sweet spice and nard. Papa had been washed and his body wrapped in the shroud. His hands and feet had been bound with strips of white cloth. The rabbi stood at Papa's feet and prayed.

Picking up Simon, Mama told him how proud he made Papa and how much Papa loved him. She spoke of some of Simon's deeds, like helping sweep the floors and how happy that made his father. She brought him near and let him touch Papa's face. Leaning over, Simon kissed his cheek and said, "I love you, Papa."

Handing Simon to me, she lifted Rachel into her arms and said, "Papa saw how beautiful you are inside and out. He was honored to be your father. He looked forward every day to eating the meals you helped to prepare. Oh, how he loved you." Mama then lowered Rachel to the floor near Papa. She took his face in her hands and stared at him. After a long moment, she cried, "Don't go away, Papa. I love you." Mama whispered in her ear, then Rachel leaned over and kissed him. Returning my sister to Jesus, Mama continued the ritual with each of us.

When it was Jesus's turn, he stepped to Papa's side, looked at him, and his heart broke. Tears poured from his eyes as he tried to speak, but all his lips could do was tremble. For several minutes, we all stood solemnly. Touching Papa's cheek, Jesus leaned over and kissed his forehead. Wiping the tears from his eyes with the sleeve of his tunic, Jesus turned and looked at us.

"One day we will be reunited, and we will gather before the throne of Almighty God. This man will sit in a place of honor. Little will be known of him, but great will be his name, for he humbly embraced what was not his as though it were."

The rabbi stopped praying and looked at Jesus with a mixture of surprise and annoyance. "I must speak with you," he said. But Jesus did not respond or move. Unaccustomed to being ignored, the rabbi said, "Now."

Without turning his attention from us or Papa, Jesus said, "I will meet with you later. Now we must bury our dead." Without another word, the rabbi again prayed.

Brushing Papa's hair, Mama stared longingly at him and kissed his forehead. Jesus stepped up and handed her the sudarium. Unfolding it, she placed it over his face. "Call in our relatives and neighbors. It will soon be time to go." A seat was placed at Papa's feet for Mama. The sound of voices grew as family and friends arrived.

A hush gradually fell over the courtyard as Jesus came out of the house. "Thank you for honoring our home. This is a day of deep sorrow, for we have been separated from our father, husband, and friend. But it is also a time of great joy, for he is with our heavenly Father, and one day we will again be together." Moving to the side and holding the door, he said, "Please come."

Many came to say their farewells and greet Mama. Afterward, Jesus and I, along with several of our cousins, lifted the litter and began our trek to the community tomb cut into the side of Nazareth Ridge. As we progressed, various family and friends took their turn carrying Papa as a sign of love and respect. When we arrived, only the family, along with the rabbi, entered the tomb.

⌒⫯⌒

A clap of thunder reverberated along the walls, jarring me back to the pile of rubble where I had found a few moments of peace. I must have fallen asleep. Rubbing the haze from my eyes, I searched the avenue for signs of life. I was alone. Checking the ground around me to avoid anything sharp, I pushed myself onto my feet and noticed something shiny under a broken table leg. A child-sized gold ring, its crest engraved with a menorah, glistened among the rubble. Slipping it into my pocket, I stood, leaned against the wall, and moved my limbs to test their strength and limitation. Pushing away from the wall, I nearly fell forward as I headed toward the Lower City.

Just before the corner at the end of the wall that surrounded Herod's palace, the sound of voices prompted me to stop. The voices grew louder and closer. Panic rose in my chest. Should I run on legs that could barely hold me up or hide in plain sight? Could I survive another encounter with Rome's cadre?

Two members of the Temple Guard turned the corner a few feet in front of me. Startled, they stepped back and brought their lances down at my chest. "Who are you?" the larger of the two said as he assumed a combat stance. "What do you want here?"

"I am going to the Lower City to find my family," I said.

"What is your name?" the other said.

"James of Nazareth. Son of Joseph, the carpenter."

Looking at me intently, he said, "Do you know the Nazarene who was put to death today by Pilate's decree?"

"He is my brother."

While the one prepared for battle and held his position, the other moved near him and whispered into his ear. A brief conversation ensued, and they came to an agreement.

"You're coming with us," they said, almost in unison.

Turning me in the opposite direction of my destination, we proceeded toward the temple, one guard ahead and the other behind me. I wondered where we headed and what were they going to do with me—or to me. Nothing good. Of that I was sure. As we navigated the abandoned streets and narrow walkways, only the rhythmic click of the guards' metal cleats against the cobblestone pavement broke the silence.

Nearing the bridge that led to the entrance along the western wall of the temple, lightning silhouetted the Xystus against the opaque sky. The open terrace and pillar-supported roof came into clear view. A number of figures milled about the veranda. They stopped and turned their attention to us when we approached. We halted short of the walkway leading to the terrace. The larger guard behind me moved himself between me and the walkway as the other ascended to the terrace and spoke to some of the people.

When he returned, he said, "We are to wait here."

"What's this about?" I said. "I've done nothing wrong. I'm only trying to find my family."

"Quiet," the smaller guard said. "Someone wants to see you."

After several minutes, a tall man dressed in the priestly garments of a synagogue leader stepped from a secluded area in the back corner of the terrace As he advanced, those on the terrace parted to give him passage. Standing at the top of the walkway, he looked me over and said, "What is your name, and where are you from?"

"My name is James, son of Joseph. I am from Nazareth."

"Do you know the Nazarene named Jesus?"

I knew I might regret my answer, but I was tired of running. "He is my brother."

Dropping my head, I took a deep breath, expecting some accusation of blasphemy or rebellion followed by the pronouncement of my guilt and the levying of the prescribed punishment.

Looking up again at my accuser, I saw a small hand reach from behind him and take hold of his robe. Tugging on it, the face of the young girl from the market peeked around at me and looked up into the tall man's face. Leaning over, he listened to her for a few moments before he stood. He continued to look at me strangely, then he beckoned with his hand and said, "Come up here."

The two guards stepped away and allowed me to ascend the walkway. At the top, I stopped. What should I do next? Surveying the audience on the terrace, I was stunned when the young girl darted from behind him, ran to me, wrapped her arms around my waist, and cried.

The man in the priestly garment walked over to me, and without warning, he wrapped his arms around my shoulders and pulled me close. To my surprise, he cried as well. The people on the porch chattered among themselves. I simply stood, my arms at my side.

Slowly, the man released me. Touching the girl's shoulder, he leaned down to her. "Come, dear, let us get our friend some water and food." Taking her hand, he looked at me and smiled. With tears running down his cheeks, he said, "Please, sit with us. You need rest and food. Come."

As the man led me across the terrace, some of the people cleared a table and some placed large cushions around it. Others brought water, bread, fruit, and fish, then they all retreated to other areas on the veranda and resumed their conversations.

"You and your brother have given me the most precious gift of all," the man said.

"We did? What gift did we give you?"

"The life of my daughter. She told me what you did in the marketplace. How you saved her life."

"We were both blessed. God had his hand on us."

"Yes, God has returned my daughter to me," he said. "Twice."

"Twice? I'm sorry I don't understand."

"A year ago, she had a fever and was sick for a long time," he said. "I sought help from every physician I could find. I prayed continually, made offerings, and sought counsel at the temple, but she remained ill and was getting worse."

Reaching around the girl's shoulders, he drew her to his side and again tears appeared in his eyes. I watched this flood of joyful emotion without comment. It was a refreshing change on this day of sorrow and pain.

Holding her close, he looked at me. "She died."

His words pierced me just as an immense bolt of lightning crossed the afternoon sky and a low rumble shook the pillars of the Xystus. I sat speechless, trying to reconcile what he had said in my mind.

"I'm sorry, what did you say?"

"My daughter's health never improved. Her sickness continued to grow worse. Finally, she died."

Realizing my mouth hung open in stunned silence, I stammered, "She died? I'm sorry . . . I don't understand."

Smiling at his daughter, he released his grip. "Her illness was too severe. Nothing could be done. But I had heard of a prophet who was proclaiming God's favor upon his people, and whose words were being affirmed by miraculous signs and wonders. I went and listened and heard the truth of the scriptures being taught. The prophet spoke with understanding, with a wisdom I had never heard."

Taking a sip of water, he continued, "I watched as he healed the blind and the lame. He cast out spirits from the demon-possessed and restored joy and peace to the hearts of the oppressed. All he did was bring healing and hope to those he touched. He asked for nothing for himself."

Leaning over the table, he put his face in his hands. "I had lost all hope. I went to him and begged him to come and heal my daughter, but it was too late. She died while I was absent." His chest and shoulders heaved as he wept, and every voice on the terrace went silent.

A servant discreetly stepped to his side and placed a small cloth over his hand, then quickly stepped away. With it, the priest wiped his eyes and said, "I am sorry for my emotions, but I cannot think of that moment without feeling the pain." Looking down at his daughter, he said, "I would have given my life and all that I have for just one more day with my beautiful girl." He leaned over and kissed her head. "Go get our guest some more water."

We watched her as she walked away, then he turned to me and said, "I was told that there was no need to seek the prophet's help, that she was dead. The mourners were at my home and preparations were being made for her burial."

He gazed out over the courtyard that lay before the terrace, took a deep breath, and continued. "My heart broken, I was about to leave when the prophet said that he would come with me. Although she lay dead, he spoke to her, raised her up, and gave her back to me. She had been dead, but now she is alive."

He leaned forward and looked into my eyes. "Only God can do such things."

Seeing the doubt on my face, he looked around at the others. "It is true. Others witnessed it, and some of them are here. Please, go and speak with them; they will tell you what happened."

Reaching across the table, he grasped my hand. "Your brother, Jesus, is the prophet of God. He has come to bring peace and hope. I believe what they say about him, that he is the Son of God."

My mind swirled. What he said about my brother was outside the realm of reason—insane to even imagine. How could my brother be God? I needed rest, and I needed time to think.

Gathering my wits, I reached into the pocket of my robe and retrieved the gold ring. With a squeal of delight, the girl reached out her hand, and I dropped it into her palm.

Her father said, "Thank you again. We thought we had lost it forever. That was my ring when I was a boy. Do you remember when we met?"

"We met before?"

"Yes. I accompanied my father to your home when your father died. My father was the rabbi who came to help in your father's burial."

"I remember you," I said.

"My father spent some time with your brother and spoke often of him. He believed Jesus was a prophet, but we weren't allowed to discuss the matter openly because such words could cause your family or mine some difficulty."

Calling an aide, the man told him to prepare a place for me to sleep. "Oh no," I said. "Thank you, but I must find my family. I have delayed too long. Thank you for the food and drink and hospitality."

Getting to my feet, I felt revitalized. Jairus stood, took my hand, and pulled me to him. Kissing my cheek, he said, "I thank God and praise Him for you and your brother. You have given me a most precious gift. You have given my daughter back to me."

Turning back at the end of the walkway, I waved farewell. Jairus called after me, "There is nothing impossible for God, my friend. The power of life is in His hands. One day you will know that power."

While he was saying this, a synagogue leader came and knelt before him and said, "My daughter has just died. But come and put your hand on her, and she will live." Jesus got up and went with him, and so did his disciples.
Matthew 9:18–19

CHAPTER NINE

Brother and Lord

Slivers of yellow light streaked across the cobblestones cast from splintered openings in shuttered windows. These subtle shafts of glimmering light provided me a dreamlike guide along the obscure path. The opaque gloom of the sunless afternoon seemed to set the appropriate mood.. Yet, as I walked along nearly abandoned streets, the sounds of conversation, prayer, and laughter emanated from behind wooden doors as families gathered for the evening meal.

How strange that an optimistic and joyful atmosphere could exist behind these wooden doors while a short distance away misery and despair flowed like a river through the streets. The dark clouds hung in the sky like a Bedouin's tent, blocking out the sun. I walked in the dim light furnished by glowing lamps that shined through broken window shutters and open doorways. Sporadic lightning crackling across the heavens offered an occasional view of what lay ahead.

Along the cobblestoned path, I overheard what sounded like conversations about the day's events. I hovered near several doors and windows to discern what was said without risking detection. From the few exchanges I heard, no one mourned for the criminals who hung on Golgotha's crosses.

Shuffling up the steep incline of a poorly maintained corridor, I staggered like a drunkard to keep my balance. At the top, I stepped out from between two tattered buildings and entered the intersection. To my left, a dirt path zigzagged through a series of deteriorating thatched houses. To my right, a more compacted clay alleyway wove past courtyard walls. In front of me, the cobblestones disappeared as they merged into a field of rooftops sprouting from the earth like wheat. In the distance, I saw the western wall of the temple. Just on the other side was the Court of the Gentiles. Would Mama and Mariam be there?

I stood motionless as I debated whether the Temple Mount should be my next stop. A group of men to my right interrupted the silence on the otherwise deserted walkway. One held a torch as the other two huddled around him near a pull cart filled with honed wooden planks. A lone figure sat next to the cart, his back against the wall. The group passed among them a clay jug—probably filled with wine. Their voices rose in a chorus of shouts, each man attempting to dominate the others, not with reason or logic but volume.

Not wanting to draw their attention, I turned away and set my focus on the wall. Within a few steps, I stopped, frozen by what I heard. The men's passionate debate had altered course, and their incensed conflict became mutual agreement as they discussed what had transpired earlier in the day.

I moved back against the wall and listened.

"They were all troublemakers," one claimed, then snorted. "I say they got what they deserved."

"Two were thieves, I was told, and the other some kind of revolutionary," another said.

"Revolutionary?" the man with the torch said. "No, no, he was a thief like the others. He's the one who went into the temple court where the merchants set up their tables, beat them with a whip, and stole their money."

"Yes, yes, that's right," agreed his companion. "I heard about that. He went in with a gang, defiled the temple, and stole everything the merchants had. If it hadn't been the Sabbath, the whole lot of them would've been executed then and there."

"Like I said, they got what they deserved," repeated the first man.

The storm continued to rumble above me as a new storm rose within me. Turning toward the group, I walked slowly but deliberately toward them. I don't know what propelled me to confront the misfits, but it was not common sense. A voice deep inside told me to ignore the boisterous windbags and move on, but another much louder one drove me forward.

"You're all wrong," I called out. "Nothing of the kind took place in the temple."

Turning their heads, they stared at me. The one holding the jug said, "How would you know? People who were there told me exactly what happened."

"No one was beaten, and nothing was taken."

The loudest of the lot, the one with the torch, stepped toward me. "We didn't have to be there. We know what happened, and the thief has gotten what he deserved!"

"None of you were there!" I shouted. "I talked with some who were there, and they said he didn't hit anyone. Nothing was taken because the man is not a thief."

The tall, thin man sitting against the wall stood and looked over the heads of the others. "You weren't there either, so how do you know he's not a thief?"

"I just know!" I said, "He would never take anything that wasn't his."

"Did you know him? Were you a part of his band?" he barked.

"No, but I knew him," I answered. "I'm his brother, and I know what happened. He made a whip, and he used it to make people move, but he didn't hit anyone with it. Yes, he overturned the money tables. But if anything was taken, someone else committed the theft."

One said, "You are the brother of the thief. Did you come to steal from us too?"

"Maybe you should be on that hill!" another snarled. They separated and moved around me.

"We know what to do with thieves," the tall, thin man said, pushing me against the cart. Attempting to turn and catch myself, I stumbled backward into the cart bed and landed on my back. My weight was more than the cart could bear, so it tipped backward, spilling me onto the ground and scattering planks across the cobblestones.

As I lay on my back in the pile of wood, an eerie silence settled around us. Shifting slowly to avoid any sudden movement that might agitate my attackers, I turned and looked up. To my relief, my new acquaintances had lost interest in me; instead, they stared at something in the distance. I turned to see what caught their attention. In the darkness stood the unmistakable outline of a Roman soldier. Around him, I counted six or seven more.

Wearied in mind and body, I fell back against the boards and closed my eyes. I inhaled the sweet aroma of cedar and thought of my childhood home.

⌒⌁⌒

The morning sun shined brightly through the window. I flinched and squeezed my eyelids shut as I pulled the heavy, draped material back from the opening. Working my way through benches, tools, and unfinished projects to the window on the opposite wall, I pulled back its curtain, allowing a light breeze to blow across the room.

The smell of wood dust filled the air like a perfumed bouquet. The fragrances of shittimwood from the acacia tree, olivewood from Bethlehem, and the leathery whiff of imported mahogany drifted through Papa's shop. The strongest scent in the room was the one I loved the most—the earthy sweetness of cedar, which generated warm memories and good feelings. God must like the aroma of cedar too, I thought, because he directed King Solomon to line the temple with it.

As the light flooded in, I surveyed all the completed work. Tables, stools, and benches were stacked in the back. Frames for what would become leather travel boxes waited for a tanner to finish the work so their prospective owners could pick them up. Some unfinished projects covered the floor; others were stacked along the walls. Papa was the finest carpenter in all Israel. Everyone, from our neighbors to the priests in Jerusalem, admired his craftsmanship. Even the Romans favored his skill in building and repair. And he had passed on his craft to my brothers and me.

All tradesmen and men of craft were instantly recognizable by the symbols they wore. Papa proudly put a wood chip behind his ear, which signified he was a carpenter by trade. My heart swelled with pride when people told him how satisfied they were with his workmanship. Sometimes he put a chip behind one of my brother's ears or mine, then patted us on the head and said, "One day you will be the carpenters, and your craftsmanship will be far superior to mine."

All my life I dreamt of what I would do, where I would go. Staying in Nazareth, except for the occasional excursion to Bethany or Jerusalem, wasn't what I had in mind. I loved Papa and appreciated all he taught me about the crafting of wood, but carpentry was not my dream. I did not want to be known as a maker of farm tools, yokes, winnowing forks, door frames, kitchen utensils, and children's dolls. I longed to explore distant horizons, and this small workshop didn't lead to any of them. Yet here I was.

A new scent mingled with the cedar—a familiar, warm smell that spoke of love and tenderness. Behind me, Mama's gentle voice said, "James, come and eat."

On the table in the courtyard, Mama placed a pitcher of water and a mug. A slice of her bread gave off that mouth-watering, freshly baked aroma. Looking at me with her usual smile, she also placed a small cup of honey on the table. "There, now eat."

"Mama!" Jesus said. "We must go if we are going to get to Cana on time."

"Yes, yes," Mama said. "I'm ready." She turned back to me. "We'll return tomorrow, James."

"Please be careful. The roads are dangerous."

"We're not going alone, brother. Some of my companions are coming," Jesus said. "Come, Mama, we must go."

Then I felt confident. Mama's safety was not only in the hands of my elder brother, but as added security, a small group of Jesus's fishermen friends would accompany her.

Spreading some honey on a piece of bread, I poured a cup of water and stepped onto the dusty roadway that passed in front of the courtyard entrance of our home. Biting into the sweet honey and warm bread, I watched as Mama and her band of protectors faded from view.

I was content to stay home. I had no interest in attending anyone's wedding. Most of those celebrations were little more than opportunities for people to catch up on family news and recent gossip. They provided little amusement for a young man. Apart from the lively music and dancing, nothing interesting would happen.

"Is this the home of Joseph the carpenter?" a low voice said behind me.

Turning, I came face to face with a member of the temple guard in full uniform. Next to him was a small, rather pale man clad in a tan robe wrapped with a brightly hued blue-and-purple sash. "Is this the home of Joseph the carpenter?" the guard repeated.

"Yes," I said. "I am James, the son of Joseph. How may I help you?"

Stepping forward, the little man said, "I am Sergius. My master instructed me to seek the services of Joseph of Nazareth, the carpenter."

"I am sorry, but my father is no longer with us. He went to be with our forefathers a year ago. How may I be of service?"

Turning to the guard, Sergius said, "Go to my master and tell him the son of Joseph will begin the work. If he does not wish him to do so, return and we will seek another carpenter."

The guard retreated past the courtyard wall and disappeared.

Removing a small scroll tucked into his sash, Sergius said, "May I have some water?"

"Yes, please sit here." I led him to a bench that sat alongside an oblong table, which our family used for everything from games and teachings to dinners and evening prayers. "I will get you water," I said and entered the house to retrieve a goblet.

Returning to the courtyard, I took a deep breath of crisp morning air. Placing the goblet in front of my guest, I filled it to the brim with fresh water, something I knew he would appreciate. The pure drink was a rarity in much of Judea.

It was a magnificent morning. The sun hovered just over the horizon, casting rays of light across a deep blue sky. Wild narcissus blossoms gave a sweet fragrance while the sound of birds and children at play filled the air. Yet this frail man seemed to find little joy in its beauty.

Leaning on his elbows, he raised the sleeve of his tunic to shade his face and block the sun from his eyes. Looking up from his makeshift shelter, he smiled slightly. "Forgive me. I have not been well." He took a sip of water, then continued. "My master needs a sella."

A sella curulis was a chair with an oblong seat covered with fine fabrics over lamb's wool. Its legs formed a wide X and could be folded, which made the chair large enough to be comfortable yet flexible enough to move with relative ease.

Sergius unfolded the scroll on the table, then pushed it in front of me so I could get a better view. "These symbols are to be inscribed upon its legs. My master heard of the quality of your father's work, and he wants these markings clearly visible." Looking intently into my eyes, he said, "Do you understand?"

"Yes," I said and turned the scroll to examine the symbols. A sella could be extremely ornate, but according to the drawing, this one would be simple and sturdy.

The symbols included a mezuzah, the reminder of God's presence; a menorah, that spoke of God's power; and the Magen David, a reminder of our heritage. Below each item was *Chai*, the Hebrew word for living.

These were not the typical cyphers engraved on a sella, but considering the request came from someone who had sent a servant accompanied by a member of the Temple Guard, I realized the markings were not unusual. The peculiar part of the request was that a sella curulis was not normally found in the possession of an Israelite, let alone a member of the temple. This particular piece of furniture was more often found in secular and nonreligious courts of power. The quality of its workmanship and cost of the materials signaled authority and influence. This was particularly true for those serving in the military. This drawing of a sella was of Roman composition yet also honored Jewish religious belief.

I wanted to know the motive for the chair's construction, but the journey to Nazareth had taken a toll on the feeble man who sat at my table. His eyes reflected the kind of void that comes when pain saps all hope from a man's heart. He was as pale as day-old milk, frail as a burnt candlewick.

He leaned toward me. "Can you fashion what my master wants? Can you do it quickly? I must return with it."

"You want me to build it now?" It would not be a lengthy undertaking, but I usually completed work in the order received.

"Yes," he said. "My master treats me with great respect and affection. He asks little, but what he asks I intend to accomplish."

"It will take some time to build it, and to engrave the characters, I will need another man's assistance," I said. "Why not return home and get the rest you require? When the sella is finished, I will deliver it myself."

He lowered his face into his hands, and his reply was muffled. "No. My master has made a simple request of me, and I intend to fulfill it." Lifting his head, he looked around the courtyard and spotted a cot in the corner. "I will rest there, and I will pay for any food or drink you provide. But I will not leave without the sella."

"I must get to work then," I said and picked up the scroll. "Please make yourself as comfortable as you can. I will get you some bread and honey now, then prepare other food later." Turning from my guest, I stepped into Papa's shop and looked at the different woods. I would need the best—no knots or blemishes.

The sella was not a large commission, and if it had been ordered by a merchant or nomad, I could have completed it in a couple of hours. But for a man of station, and for the quality expected, additional attention to detail and craftsmanship would be required. I planned to have it cut and assembled by morning.

The one most skilled in the art of inscription and scoring would not be available until the next day, because that was when my brother would return. If I remained diligent through the night, the chair would be ready by midday for Jesus to engrave the symbols and apply a smooth, hand-rubbed olive oil finish. If all went according to plan, this sick man could then return home and present the meticulously crafted piece to his master.

"Brother." The voice was soft and the hand on my shoulder was gentle, but I awoke with a start, sitting up abruptly from an uncomfortable position. A sharp pain darted through my aching limbs, and I rubbed the kinks and stiffness from my neck.

"Who is the man on the cot?" Jesus said. "He doesn't look well."

"I believe he came from the temple. He is waiting for a sella curulis to take to his master," I said, pointing to the chair on the worktable. "He wants symbols, Jewish symbols, engraved on the legs."

Stepping to the table, Jesus examined the sella. "You have done well, little brother. Papa would have been proud." Turning his attention to the scroll that lay next to the chair, he said, "Is this what they wish?"

"Yes. A sella curulis is Roman, isn't it? Yet the symbols are Jewish. Why would anyone in the temple want such a thing?"

"It will not be in the temple," Sergius said, standing in the open doorway. "The responsibility of my master's command requires him to travel often between Jerusalem and Capernaum. He desires a durable, light seat so he can take it to each post."

With the morning light shining behind him, our guest had a surprisingly healthier countenance.

"A little rest and a little food have done you well," I said. With a slight nod and smile, he agreed.

"This is my brother," I said, motioning toward Jesus. "He will engrave the symbols for you this afternoon, and your project will be oiled and completed. Then you can be on your way."

"Thank you. My master will be pleased," he said and turned away from the door. "I will wait out here in the sun's invigorating warmth."

I watched him leave and reflected on his condition from the previous day. He had been weak and anemic. "You would not believe how ill he was yesterday, but today it's as if he was never sick at all." I shook my head. "And I don't understand why his master would want a Roman seat of authority adorned with symbols that speak of the God of Israel."

Jesus lifted the sella from the table and laid it on its side. Reaching for an engraving chisel, he wore the smile that said he knew something I didn't. "God's representation can be engraved on much more than Roman furniture, little brother. It can be etched upon the Roman heart as well."

◦⤬◦

A rumble of thunder growled low and deep as a whiff of cedar brought me back from the memories of Papa's shop. Another growl came low and deep, but this time it came with the words, "What are you doing?"

I groaned and lifted my head to see who spoke. I saw the tall, thin man, the one who propelled me into the cart, the man holding a torch, and another holding a wine jug. They all stood as still as pillars, looking back toward the intersection in the direction from where I had come.

At the end of the alleyway stood a soldier in polished armor and crowned with a transverse crest on his helmet, indicating he was a senior commander, a centurion of considerable rank. The other four soldiers were younger. Two held torches in one hand, and all held lances. All were fully equipped for battle with broadswords and daggers tightly secured at their hip. Behind them walked two unarmed men who appeared to be men of station by the quality of their dress.

"What's going on here?" commanded the centurion.

"We caught a thief," responded one of the four men.

"Yes, yes, a thief," the others chimed in.

"What was he stealing, a cart of wood scraps?" said the centurion.

"No. He's the brother of the thief who stole from our temple," one of the four responded.

"Being a brother of a thief doesn't make a man a thief," the centurion said. "So why is he being punished for what his brother did? Go get his brother."

"His brother already received what he deserved." The man with the torch snickered. "He's one of the thieves you nailed to a cross today."

"You sure put him where he belongs," the tall, thin man said.

"You sure did," another said. "Right in the middle." Patting each on the back, they all laughed.

The centurion stepped forward and gave them a look that sent chills down my back. "It's late. It's time for you to go home. Enjoy your religious feast while you still can."

"We don't take part in all that stuff," the man with the jug said. "Some of us don't even have a home to go to."

Taking another step toward them, the centurion spoke low but clearly as the other soldiers moved into a flanking position around the four men. "Find somewhere to go . . . and go now."

Their smug arrogance and defiance morphed into timid compliance as the four vanished into the darkness of the alleyway.

Coming up onto my knees, I struggled to stand. Strong hands grasped my arms from both sides and lifted me like a bag of wheat. On my feet, I attempted to step away, but the two soldiers tightened their grip. Leaning forward, the centurion placed his face close to mine. Would I leave the alleyway alive?

His voice was low and intimidating. "You are the brother of the Nazarene? The one who was crucified today?"

A shrill inner voice screamed, *No! I don't even know who he is!* But I remained silent. Thoughts marched through my mind: *Thieves get crucified, and I am no thief,* or *Yes, and proud of it.* My legs went weak with the thought of being nailed to a cross, and standing close enough to feel his breath was one who could make sure that happened.

Retreating slightly, he signaled for the two young legionnaires to release me. I slumped against the wall. Mama was going to lose another son. My only hope now was a quick death by a Roman lance.

"We were not part of the tribunal or its results," the centurion said. With a wave of his hand, he dismissed his men. "Leave us."

The young soldiers walked briskly to the intersection and disappeared around the corner. The two nonmilitary figures remained. One retreated to the intersection and stood at the corner while the other stepped to the centurion's side.

"I asked you a question," the centurion said. "Are you the brother of the Nazarene who was crucified today?" he said with the same slow snarl he'd used with the four rabble-rousers.

Lifting my eyes to meet his gaze, I said as emphatically as I could, "Yes . . . he is my brother."

His eyes seemed to soften. I may have seen a tear form, but it was dark, and torchlight can be deceiving.

Reaching around, he took the elbow of the man at his side and drew him close. "This man is my family. He has been at my side all my life. His father served my father, and he has served me faithfully."

I knew this man. His blue-and-purple sash was tightly wrapped around fine, white linen this time, not the tan, coarse wool he had worn when I first met him. He seemed taller, even heavier, and his eyes expressed hope and real happiness.

"Sergius," I said, extending my hand.

Pushing my hand aside, he stepped forward and put his arms around me. "Hello, James." The strength of his embrace surprised me. I had seen this man reenergized by a night's rest, but this was something else. This was the renewing of the whole man.

"I thought I would lose this man who is so close to my heart." The centurion's voice was laced with wonder. "Illness would not release its grip on my dear friend. For years

I sought the wisdom of those who care for kings, but they held no power over death."

Placing his hand on Sergius's shoulder, he continued. "Then I called upon the one I should have been seeking all along, and by the power of his word, my friend stands with us now."

Sergius patted the centurion's hand and looked heavenward with an ear-to-ear smile.

Although I appreciated the opportunity to see this man in such excellent health and to hear the wonderful report of his healing, I needed to be on my way. "Thank you for your assistance, but I must be going." I said, reaching for Sergius's hand. "And it is good to see you again, and to hear of your recovery."

Not knowing if I was going to be detained, I turned to the centurion. "May I go?" I lowered my head in respect for his authority. "I must continue my search for my mother and sister. They grieve for my brother."

"Yes, by all means," he said. "I mourn with you, for your loss and mine."

"Your loss?"

"The man who died this day on that cross—you know him as your brother . . . I know him as my Lord."

When Jesus had entered Capernaum, a centurion came to him, asking for help. "Lord," he said, "my servant lies at home paralyzed, suffering terribly." Jesus said to him, "Shall I come and heal him?" The centurion replied, "Lord, I do not deserve to have you come under my roof. But just say the word, and my servant will be healed."

Matthew 8:5–8

CHAPTER TEN

With Eyes to See

On limbs that had been abused in a body that had been beaten, I returned to that abhorrent hill where my brother breathed his last. Mama would not have left him. Why had I thought she would?

I marveled at how diverse these lonely streets were and how quickly their character could change. Gone was the elation of the Passover celebration and the sweet melody of children at play. The murmur of prayers emitting from every doorway also was gone.

The sounds that earlier echoed off those masonry walls had faded too. Sounds of hatred and anger, cries that demanded retribution for an unwitnessed offense, an unverified transgression. Also missing were the shouts from a mob whose consciences had been dulled by their ignorance and their blood lust.

The silence was a welcome reprieve.

With every step I took, that dreadful mound of earth drew closer. Although I could not see it, the images of what I had run from flooded my mind. My pace slowed as I debated whether to continue. I began to rationalize and create reasons why I didn't need to return to Golgotha. Mama may not even be there now. I saw him die. What would be the point of staying?

The lightning's rolling radiance through the clouds had slackened, leaving the street dark and difficult to navigate. I slid my hand over the wall and the shutters, feeling my way along the cobblestone pathway.

From one splinter of light emanating from shuttered windows to the next, I moved, my hand lightly touching the wall to provide some measure of assurance I was on track. Was it necessary to return to Golgotha, to gaze upon the grisly results of Rome's contemptuous expression of justice? My pace slowed even further as the images of my brother's execution flitted through my mind. His face unrecognizable; his body beaten and abused. The crowd's hateful taunts. His anguished cries. And Mama's. And Mariam's.

Engulfed in the shadows where no shuttered windows emitted slats of light, I stopped, pressed my forehead against a wall, and sobbed. I couldn't take another step. I didn't have the strength. My resolve had dissolved into self-pity and regret.

Hearing voices, I looked up to see a torchlight coming from the direction of the Gennath Gate. In the dim light, I made out the figures of several homeless street dwellers sitting along the wall. Not wanting another confrontation, I sat along the wall next to them as two men approached, one carrying a torch.

"I don't understand it. Who asked for him? It is outside of the permitted distance from the city wall, so why take him now?" said the shorter man with the torch.

"I heard a rich man from Arimathea asked for him," said the taller one. "I don't know much more than that."

"Well, perhaps now there'll be peace. He was nothing but a disrupter anyway."

As they passed, the other said, "He is not a problem anymore, and I do not intend to involve myself any further. Like Pilate, I wash my hands of the whole matter."

A bolt of brilliant white shot through the clouds directly over the Tower of Hippicus, striking the ground somewhere outside the western wall. The street grew dark again as the two men and their torch disappeared. Sitting in the darkness, I thought of the first time I looked up at that great tower.

⊶∞⊷

"That, little brother, is the Tower of Hippicus, and the one on the left is the most beautiful—the Tower of Mariamne," Jesus said with a twinge of excitement. "In the back is the tallest tower, the Tower of Phasael."

I enjoyed coming to Jerusalem with my brother because he named the various structures and described them so well. Sometimes, though, his breadth of knowledge was irritating. As a boy, I thought he was making up a lot of the details because he seemed to know so much. But in time I realized that he loved this city and studied it carefully.

"King Herod built these towers and the wall to fortify and protect the city and his palace from anyone attacking it from the west. It sits on one of the highest places in the land," Jesus said. "Come, I want to show you something."

Leading the way, he stopped short of the Gennath Gate that would have led us out of the walled city. "Isn't it beautiful?" He turned, and the joy on his face had turned to sadness. "If only it had always been so, and if only it would always be."

"What? It has always been beautiful, and it will last forever," I countered.

"Yes, brother, Jerusalem will last forever," he said, patting my shoulder. "But like the rose of Sharon, its beauty will fade. In due time, though, it will return more beautiful than before."

"Sometimes you speak in riddles," I said, irritated. "Look around you." He often spoke as though he knew something the rest of us did not, but this time he was clearly off the mark. Placing my hand on a giant stone at the base of the wall, I said, "These stones have been here for hundreds of years. Our ancestors walked by and touched them. If they cannot be moved, how can they or their beauty ever fade?"

He smiled, turned, and continued through the gate. Stopping under the archway, we looked out across the magnificent Pool of the Towers. Almost sixty paces wide and one hundred paces long, its waters glimmered in the afternoon sun.

"The king of Assyria sat there," Jesus said, pointing to a raised slab of rock between two pillars. "There he met with King Hezekiah almost seven hundred years ago."

"Of course you know who was here and when," I said with an eye roll. "And you even know where they sat."

"Listen in synagogue during Passover when we're here," he said, "and to Papa and Mama during our morning and evening prayers. You miss so much by letting your mind wander to places you will never be that you do not learn about the places you will go."

Shoved violently across the archway, I turned to see my brother pushed in the opposite direction. The force caused him to fall forward down the first two steps that led to the pool. A man clothed in dirty rags, his long hair and beard matted in mud, stumbled down the steps and fell at the bottom, just short of the pool.He scrambled to his feet and ran, flailing his arms and grunting like a wild animal.

With each step, he stumbled as he ran alongside the pool, hands grasping the air, head continually turning as though he was looking for something. At the pool's edge, he spun around, arms outstretched, hands opening and closing frantically as though he was seeking something to hold on to. His head went back, his eyes widened, and he stared directly into the sun. From his mouth came a shrill howl like a tortured creature in pain. Losing his balance, he fell, striking his head on the stone edge of the pool and rolling into the water.

The man flung his limbs wildly, disappearing under the churning water, then reappearing to cry out and gasp for air. Jesus ran toward the man, pulling off whatever garments he could before reaching the pool's edge. Jumping in, he grabbed the man and lifted him above the water. Although the pool was shallow—no higher than a man's chest—the man fought with such panic that he pulled them both under the surface several times.

I ran to the side of the pool and watched as this madman did his absolute best to drown himself and my brother. But the battle was exhaustive, and soon the man grew still. Taking hold of the man's robe and stepping back, Jesus pulled him to a stone step that ran along the pool's edge, just below the surface. Together, we lifted him onto the flat stone. He lay still, eyes closed, breathing deeply.

"This man must be possessed," I said.

"No. He is confused and frightened," Jesus said as he cradled the man's head in his arm and brushed the hair from his face. "Fold my robe and place it underneath his head, then we'll lift him out of the pool."

A small crowd had gathered. Looking at the poor wretch with curiosity and disdain, I said to the people closest to us, "Please help us move him." No one stepped forward to help, as I expected.

On the contrary, they stepped back as one said, "We know this man. He is possessed by a demon."

"He's only confused and frightened." I parroted my brother's words, although I questioned whether he was right. Why else would this man act in such a way? Why would he look directly into the sun or make those strange sounds?

"Who are you?" I said, when he sat up. His mouth opened as if to speak, but he did not utter a word.

His head tilted upward, and he looked at me with milky white eyes. Now I understood. He stared into the sun because he could not see it.

"Yes, brother," Jesus said. "He is also mute."

Jesus placed his hands on either side of the man's face, leaned forward, and whispered something into his ear. The man turned his head toward Jesus as his wet mop of hair fell over his face. He moved his lips as if to form words, but all that came out were groans.

"What are you doing there? Leave him alone," came a voice from behind me. The large hand of a temple guard grabbed a handful of my robe and dragged me back. Another guard did the same to my brother.

A man dressed in the robes and shawl of a Pharisee stepped between us and our crazed acquaintance.

"Yosef, are you all right? Have you been hurt?" he said. "Have these men hurt you?"

He cowered when he heard the Pharisee's voice and shook his head vigorously.

"These men saved him from drowning in the pool," said one of the onlookers.

"They pulled him from the water," another said.

Motioning to the temple guards, the Pharisee said. "Help these men to their feet." A hand under my arm lifted me. "Thank you for rescuing Yosef. His parents placed him under our charge three years ago. He will return to Decapolis soon. Again, thank you."

He nodded to the guards, and they moved to either side of Yosef, then lifted him to his feet. "Bring him."

Yosef twisted out of their grasp, shrieked as though he had been struck, and frantically swung his arms. He struck one of the guards, who lost his balance and tumbled headlong into the pool. To avoid being hit, the other guard stepped back and withdrew the dagger from his belt.

"Stop!" Jesus shouted, as he moved between the dagger and Yosef.

I stood stunned, waiting for my brother to be impaled. What provoked him to act this way? Without regard for his safety, let alone mine, he often inserted himself into someone else's life or problem no matter how unwelcome or dangerous it might be.

"Stop," Jesus repeated and placed his open palm against the dagger's point. "Stop."

Yosef also stopped, his blind eyes staring off into the distance, his arms hanging limp at his side.

"Jesus, we need to go," I said. "Now."

But my brother turned his attention to the Pharisee. "With your permission, rabbi, we would like to accompany you. With your consent, we would like to walk with Yosef. I believe we have become friends, and I promise there will be no more trouble."

Looking first at the guard climbing out of the pool with hate in his eyes, then to the guard wielding the dagger, the Pharisee said, "Yes, that is an excellent idea. But I will hold you responsible for any additional disruption."

"I understand," Jesus said. "Come, brother. Let's help our friend get home."

Our friend? When did he become our friend? Again, my brother rerouted us from our desired destination and inserted us into the troubles of a newfound friend. These detours were often frustrating, but they did make life more interesting.

Jesus took Yosef's arm, and I moved cautiously to his other side, keeping a wary eye on him for any sign of another eruption. Looking over my shoulder, I smiled at the angry guard behind me. Taking the lead, the Pharisee smugly moved through the crowd as they cast aspersions at Yosef with just enough volume to be heard.

We walked around the pool parallel to the Western Wall, winding through a series of narrow streets and avenues lined with small mud huts. As we passed a hill to our left, the guard behind me said to the other, "Look, more of Rome's handywork."

On the hill and down the slope that ran along its backside were five wooden crosses. On two of them hung bodies. Even from this distance I could tell that the men had been dead for some time. My stomach lurched with nausea.

Jesus glanced at the crosses, then leaned close to Yosef and said, "You will one day see what you do not wish to see, and your tongue will utter words you do not wish to hear."

"What?" I said.

"Those words were for our friend, little brother," Jesus said.

"That doesn't sound like something you ought to be telling a friend," I said, hoping his words did not trigger another outburst.

The Pharisee led us to the front of a thatched roof hut, then leaned down and called through the small doorway. "Hello, is there anyone in there?"

A petite lady with skin as pale as ashes emerged from the shadows. "Yes, rabbi. What can I do for you?"

"I am returning your son. We can no longer control him."

A small man with the same unhealthy appearance emerged. "Why? Is he not able to do the work you require of him?"

"No, he is not. He is also becoming more violent. He just assaulted one of my temple guards," the rabbi said. "I either return him to you or take him to the Fortress of Antonia and place him in the Citadel."

"No," cried the woman. "We will take him."

The man stepped out and took Yosef by the hand. "Come, son. You are home." Together they retreated into the shadows of the small hut.

The rabbi turned to us. "I'm glad to be rid of him. Thank you for your assistance. You are dismissed."

Dismissed? If it weren't for us, you would all still be bobbing around in that pool, I thought as I watched the Pharisee and his guards march down the dusty pathway.

Jesus and I took the same route back into the city. I focused intently on the ground and my next step. I did not want to see the bodies of those men on the crosses again. Once was enough.

"Jesus, why did what you whispered in Yosef's ear calm him down so quickly?" Maybe some conversation would take my mind off what hung on that hill.

"He needed hope. So I told him that one day his eyes would see the beauty of a sunrise and his lips would praise the One who created it."

"Do you really believe that is true?"

"Yes," he said.

I looked up at him. He was staring at that sickening pile of rock, and a tear ran down his cheek.

A clap of thunder shook the ground, and several frightened shouts rang out from my fellow residents along the wall. The memory of my first sight of decaying bodies on a cross reignited my hesitancy to return to Golgotha.

I weighed out every conceivable option, but I truly had only one choice. Rising slowly, I maintained unbroken contact with the wall as my only point of reference. Taking short, deliberate steps, my hand glided over the surface of the stones, and I worked my way toward what I thought was the end of the street.

I stepped onto something soft but firm, and an angry voice called out, "Watch out, there. That's my foot."

"Sorry," I said and pulled away from the security afforded by the wall. I plotted my way; eyes wide and arms outstretched, I attempted to avoid running into a wall, a pillar, or a person. A name floated through my mind. Yosef.

This is the life he lived, I thought, but he could not even apologize for stepping on a man's foot or pushing a guard. He lived in a world of darkness filled with voices but none of them his. Sorrow mixed with gratitude stopped me. Standing in the stillness, I opened my eyes wide. Rotating slowly to my left, I extended my arms and peered into the black world around me. Making several complete rotations, I turned to my right and did it again.

I was lost. I had some knowledge of my whereabouts when I began, but now I had no idea where I was or what direction to go. Panic rose within me when I realized that, unlike Yosef, my hope was simply when the sun rose. But I could not wait for morning to find Mama, so I crept forward with the caution of the blind. Within moments, I was reunited with a wall. But was it the right wall, and was I heading in the right direction?

To my relief, after feeling my way around numerous bodies and through heaps of debris, I arrived at the crossroads of a wider, better lit avenue. From its intersection, I saw the flicker of torchlight some distance away at the entry of the Gennath Gate. Using that glint of light as a beacon, I set my course.

I walked past the Pool of the Towers and alongside the mud huts until I came to an opening that led to a dirt trail. This route would take me to where I did not wish to go. Pausing, I let my mind recapture the scene I had run from earlier. A brother, beaten and bloody on a cross, a mother witnessing the cruelty inflicted upon her firstborn son, and a sister, consoling her mother as she watched the execution of her big brother and best friend.

My pace was slow but consistent. I could just make out a rise of earth with what I assumed were the crosses on its crest. Along the path, small groups of men and women walked somberly. Had any of them left a family member or a friend on that hill? I studied each group, and each face of the women, hoping I would meet Mama and Mariam on the road and avoid the hill. Each woman passed with sorrow on her face.

The clouds billowed as lightning danced within their folds casting an illusory aura along the path and around the rise. The dull skies provided some light but hid the evening sun.

The trail narrowed around a large boulder, restricting access to the summit and concealing my view of the crosses. I stopped under the overhang and allowed several mournful groups to pass and continue down the hill. When the path was clear, I climbed the remaining thirty paces to Golgatha.

There hung Dismas, dead, and Gestas, moaning in pain, but the cross in the middle was empty. Where was he? Who had taken his body, and why would someone have taken him?

Penetrating the surreal silence were the laments and sobs of a group of women to my right. At the foot of the cross on which my brother had hung sat a solitary figure, his hands covering his face. Clothed in a tattered but clean robe, hair pulled back and tied behind his head, he sat motionless.

"Sir," I said, "Do you know what happened to the man that was put to death on this cross?"

Without looking up, he said in a voice broken with emotion, "They have taken him."

"Where?"

With one hand, he pointed behind him. "I do not know where they have taken my healer, but some of them went that way."

I surveyed the open terrain that ran from the back of the disgusting knoll toward a rock-covered ridge and peered into the gloom, searching for movement. Wherever they had taken him, Mama and Mariam would be there.

As I advanced down the backside of the hill, I wondered if it wouldn't be more prudent to search out some of those who followed Jesus. They might be able to provide suggestions or shed light on Mama and Mariam's whereabouts. An answer I had already received flooded back into my mind. *I do not know where they have taken my healer.*

"Healer," I said aloud. Were we talking about the same man, or was he referring to someone else? I ran back up the hill, hoping the man had not departed. There he sat in the same grief-stricken position.

"I want to know where they took the man that was crucified on this cross today," I said.

"I told you. I don't know."

"You said he was your healer. I'm not looking for a doctor. I'm looking for my brother, the Nazarene."

"Your brother?" he said, lifting his head.

When his gaze to meet mine, I knew. There before me sat the crazed, blind mute from the Pool of the Towers. His eyes were no longer a milky white but a deep hazel. Traces of a smile formed on his lips as his mouth opened and he spoke with clear resonance. "You are his brother?"

"Yes, Yosef, he is my brother," I said. "What has happened to you?"

"He healed me."

I remembered Yosef well. But not like this. His appearance and behavior were so radically different that it was difficult to see him as the demented man he had been.

"What do you mean he healed you?"

"He took away my pain and gave me my sight. He took away my fear and gave me my voice." Dropping his head, he wept. "And they came and took him away from me."

"Who are they, and where did they take him?"

"The centurions took his life, and a man from the Sanhedrin, along with some others, came and took his body."

What more could the Romans and religious leaders do to my family? They took my brother's life and now they have stolen his body. Driving my fist into the base of the cross, I snarled. "Where did they go? Where did they take him?"

"I don't know." His cries deepened into sobs.

My anger faded as I watched this broken man weep. He had been given a great gift but had lost a greater friend.

"Where is your family, Yosef? You should go home."

Pointing toward the city wall, he said, "My home is there, but it is empty now. Soon after the rabbi brought me home, my mother and father died. They had not been well for some time, and I was a great burden upon them."

"You should not remain here. I do not know how it happened, but you have been given an opportunity to live a different life. Go home and leave this place."

A painful groan could be heard above me. I looked up at Gestas. His legs had been broken and he hung gasping for air. It was clear that death was approaching him quickly, and for his sake, I prayed that it would be soon.

"This is a place of death, Yosef. You should not be here. Go and enjoy the gift you have received," I said.

"Do you remember what he told me? He said that one day I would see and speak, but I would see what I did not wish to see. Do you remember? He said I would speak what I did not wish to hear. I have seen, and I tell you: they have put my hope to death."

"No, no, your hope is not dead. We mourn the loss of a brother and friend, but our lives continue." I glanced at my childhood friend, whose body hung limp upon the cross.

My brother's words resonated in my mind. "We have been given the right to live wisely or foolishly. Leave this place, my friend, and live a life of gratitude for the gifts of sight and speech you have received."

Reaching down, I placed a hand under Yosef's arm and lifted him to his feet. *Who am I to be talking this way, encouraging someone else by echoing my brother's words as though they were my own?*

"I must find where they took him. My mother and sister will be with him. I cannot leave them alone any longer. Goodbye, Yosef. Be well." I proceeded down the hill, back in the direction I had come from.

Behind me came sharp, well-defined words from a voice that had rarely been heard. "He also told me that one day my eyes would see the beauty of a sunrise, and my lips would praise the one who created it. Watch for the sunrise."

Then they brought him a demon-possessed man who was blind and mute, and Jesus healed him, so that he could both talk and see. All the people were astonished and said, "Could this be the Son of David?"
Matthew 12:22–23

CHAPTER ELEVEN

The Giver of Life

Although the clouds remained, the darkness lifted, allowing for easier travel. But in the shadowed, narrow streets, torchlight would have been helpful. Moving along the western wall outside the Upper City, I ran my hand along the massive stones that generations had seen as protection against those who wished to rule over God's greatest city by force. Over my shoulder, I saw the silhouette of three crosses: one empty and two still occupied. The wall had not prevented those deaths.

At the Tower of Phasael, the top of Herod's palace rose above the city wall. Its bronze roof reflected the marbled light of a few rays of the evening sun fighting their way through the clouds. How comfortable Herod must be in his fortress as the world around him struggles. Would those in authority ever be required to live by the same rules they placed on everyone else? Why did Jerusalem's walls fail to protect us? Simple answer. Behind them lived hypocrisy.

I crept past the enormous Serpent's Pool that provided water to various pools and cisterns within the city. Around its borders, families and pilgrims from throughout Palestine had set up temporary abodes. Setting up camp there enabled them to stay within the compulsory distance of the city and the temple during the Passover celebration. Children played. Men and women clustered in family groups. All interacted joyfully. All seemed unaware that a short distance away hung two petty thieves beside an empty cross.

My heart celebrated the laughter of the children whose innocence had not yet been stolen by adult conflict. But my momentary joy was soon engulfed by the murky swamp of the day's events. Even so, the confrontations and physical abuse had reunited me with intriguing people and brought unique insights into my brother's life.

The mingled smell of bread and roasted lamb drifted through the air as I stepped around the people who reclined near the pool. Evening approached, and the heat became more bearable. Gaps in the blanket of clouds formed, allowing the setting sun to paint the horizon in vivid yellows, oranges, and burgundies. The diffused light of dusk cast an otherworldly glow across the array of encampments. If only the day had been a dream, I could awake and the nightmare would be over.

I found an opening between several men along the pool's rim and knelt to fill my palms with the cool water. Splashing it on my face, I leaned over the pool and saw the reflection of a desperately lost man. What more could this day bring? What else would assault my mind or body? What new revelation about my brother would be revealed?

My hair and beard dripped, and I looked at the men on either side of me. "Nothing," I murmured. "Nothing else they can do to me, and nothing more that can be fabricated about my brother."

"What's that?" said the man to my right.

"No more pain, and no more lies!" I shouted, thrusting my fist toward the sky.

The impulse to strip off my clothing and jump into the pool washed over me. At the edge of the water, two voices in my brain waged war. Impulse said, *Strip and jump.* Reason countered, *No, walk away. Now.* Untying my belt, I held it in my hand and stepped to the edge of the pool.

The two men sensed what was about to happen and scrambled backward. Just as I lifted my left foot, a lightning bolt crossed the sky. I gazed into the heavens, and reason defeated impulse. I looked down at the men to either side of me. "Going for a swim may not be the best idea."

Both nodded.

I turned away from the pool, wrapped my belt around my waist, and sat on the raised curb that prevented wagon wheels from slipping into the water. I scanned the various camps spread out before me. Did anyone in this makeshift city of sojourners know my brother before they condemned him? And how close to him were they who wept?

As I ambled through the labyrinth of tents and children, a young woman appeared from the perimeter of the encampment and walked back between two large tents. Walking past where she disappeared, I heard a familiar voice. "James? James, is that you?"

I turned in time to see the angelic face of a dear friend illuminated by a brilliant light that blazed across the sky.

"James?"

"That's me," I said, "Mary?"

"Yes," she said and threw her arms around my neck.

The young woman I had known since childhood was maturing into a beautiful woman. "So good to see you," I said. "What are you doing here?"

"Looking for you."

"For me?"

She glanced toward Golgotha, then met my gaze. "What they've done is horrible. Beyond understanding. He did nothing wrong." She turned and stared at the dreadful silhouette. Taking a deep breath, she said, "Your mother and sister are at our home. Please come with me. They need you."

"Of course." I released a deep sigh. My search was about to end.

After we moved past the mass of bodies and noise of encamped pilgrims, a stillness settled around us. We walked in silence. Although a thin layer of clouds remained, the evening light was sufficient to maneuver along the southern wall, through the Kidron Valley and the trees of the Mount of Olives. The lights of Bethany flickered in the distance. There I would be reunited with Mama and Mariam.

Sensing that the silence should be broken, I said, "I heard your brother, Lazarus, died. I'm sorry for your loss. He was a good friend."

"Thank you." She stopped, turned, and looked at me with an odd sense of peace. "Have you not heard what happened?"

"No. What?"

"My brother died, and we buried him, but—" She studied my face. "Never mind. Let me show you."

"Show me what?"

She shook her head and said, "Better to surprise you."

In the courtyard of the house Mary shared with her siblings sat Mama and Mariam. I had abandoned them at the most heartbreaking moment of our lives. I would not blame them if they were angry.

When Mariam saw us, she leapt to her feet, ran, and embraced me. "James, we have been so worried about you." Mama spread her arms wide, beckoning me to fill them. We sat and held one another silently. No words were necessary, but what was churning within me had to be said.

I sat back and looked into my mother's eyes. "Mama, I'm sorry," I said, my voice cracking. "Mama, please forgive me."

"Nothing to forgive. We all fled from there in our own way," she said.

Mariam kissed my cheek.

Over the next hour, Mama told me what had happened after I left. "You were not the only one who could not bear to stay. Even those closest to him fled. All but one."

Stretched out on a wooden bench, head propped on a folded sheepskin, a young man slept. I recognized him as the youngest of those who followed my brother. His name was John, the one to whom Jesus entrusted my mother's care.

Mama spoke of a kind member of the Sanhedrin who received permission to take Jesus's body and prepare it for burial in his own tomb. Others came, too, and helped with the initial preparations until his burial could be completed after the Sabbath. Mary and Martha had heard about the crucifixion after Jesus died, but they met Mama and Mariam at the tomb and encouraged them to return home with them.

In the cool evening, Martha emerged from the house with a tray of bread and cheese. "You must eat to regain your strength. I have filled the basin inside so you can wash."

Mary followed with fish and oil. "You must stay with us through the Sabbath. Please make yourself comfortable."

"May I help?" said Mariam.

"An extra pair of hands will be welcome," Martha said.

"Mary," I said, "You said you would show me something about your brother's death."

With a peculiar smile, she looked out through the courtyard entrance. "Soon. I have to finish up a few things first." She motioned to Mariam, and they returned to the house.

Mama and I sat in silence a few minutes. I held her hand while she gazed at the stars that shown through the clouds. The expression on her face was one I had seen many times as a child. I had watched her from the window above my bed when she sat in the courtyard of our home late in the evening and prayed.

I couldn't comprehend the pain of losing a child, especially the way Jesus had been taken. Although tears pooled in her eyes, she seemed to be at peace.

A web of lightning shot across the sky.

Patting her hand, I said softly, "I'm here, Mama. I'll never leave you again."

⌘

"I'm not going in there," I said when my brother and several of our friends disappeared into a hole in the side of the bluff. We had explored every crevice and cave within a mile or more of Nazareth. Thanks to recent rains, the earth had slid away and exposed a cave we had not investigated. A new cave required exploration.

I never wanted to be the first to go in. I left that to the older boys. So I waited outside, expecting to hear it was just another dark hole. Nothing exciting inside.

The caves were only deep indentations—five or ten paces deep at most. A wall-to-wall search took just a few minutes. And I could usually hear the other boys' voices and movements coming from inside. This time, however, I could not hear anything. Concerned, I stepped to the opening and peered in.

The sun had set behind the bluff, leaving the cave in darkness. I listened for sounds.

"What's in there?" Hearing only my echo in response. "Are you all right in there?" My mind raced. What do I do? Should I run for help? I stepped in, but only a few paces. Were they hurt? Should I go in alone to find them? Panic set in.My palms began to sweat and heart began to race. Go in! Of course, go in. What was I thinking?

Time seemed to stand still as I waited for my eyes to adjust to the darkness. Suddenly the air was filled with screams and shouts as the other boys raced past me toward the entrance.

"Run!" They shouted. "Run!"

I turned, shrieked, and ran until I realized I was running alone. Looking back, I saw my brother and friends laughing hysterically. Jesus bent low, holding his side.

"That's not funny," I said, striding back to the group.

"You should see it from our perspective, little brother," Jesus said, trying to catch his breath.

"What's in there?" I said.

"Nothing. We just wanted to see what you'd do," Jesus said. "You sure can move when you want to."

"I'm faster than any of you," I boasted.

"You're not that fast. Let's go back to the road, and I'll race you to the well," said Asher, always quick to respond.

"Yes, yes," all the others said.

We walked down to the well, about a mile away. I strutted ahead of the others, confident of victory.

On the road, we each lifted our robes and girded ourselves with our belts, making sure we could run without hindrance. The other boys and I lined up while Jesus removed his sandals. Unlike the rest of us, he preferred to run barefoot. He said that feeling the earth beneath him made him swifter.

Asher glared at me. "Are you ready?"

"I'm ready," I said just as he yelled, "Go!" and sprinted off.

Within moments, I caught up with Asher and passed him. He was the oldest and tallest of our friends, but he's also the slowest. After making the curve in the road, the well came into sight. I was sure of my win until my peripheral vision caught some movement to my right. With sandals in hand, my brother drew up alongside me, smiled, then passed me.

Drawing upon every ounce of strength I had left, I drove my feet into the dust, propelling myself forward. About fifty paces from our goal, I pulled ahead and reached the well moments before he did. Breathless, I bent over, hands on my knees. When I looked up, the others were walking wearily up the road, Asher trailing well behind.

Jesus dropped the bucket into the well and withdrew fresh water. Handing me the bucket, he said, "As the winner, you get the first drink. Well run, little brother."

I returned the bucket to him. He took a long drink, slipped his feet into his sandals, and gave me the customary pat on the head. "I'll see you at dinner." He turned to the exhausted posse that had gathered around the well. "Let's look for more new caves tomorrow. Maybe we'll see how fast James can move again." More laughter at my expense, but this time I joined them.

When Asher finally made it to the well, he dropped his large frame onto the ground and said, "What's everybody laughing at? Better not be me." He pulled his leg up and rubbed it. "I would have beaten all of you if my leg hadn't cramped."

"Is that the same cramp that kept you from winning last time? And the time before that?" I said. The other boys giggled.

With a scowl, Asher snapped at me like a mad dog. "Not funny. Who do you think you are anyway? Everybody knows your family isn't normal."

"What are you talking about?" I said.

"Everybody knows that Jesus isn't your brother or the son of your father." He snickered.

An uncontrollable rage rose in my chest. I jumped to my feet and charged Asher, wanting to inflict as much pain as I could. Just as I reached him, he swung his meaty paw in my direction. It landed squarely on my right eye and knocked me down. Everything went black.

I awoke in my bed with Mariam putting a cool, wet cloth on my face. "What happened?"

"Your friends said you slipped and hit the well." Placing water and food on the table next to me, she said, "I guess we should rename the well Asher. What do you think?"

"Let's not."

As she turned to leave, I said, "Mariam, have you ever heard people talk about Jesus?"

"Of course. I've heard people talk about you too. Why?"

"Asher said something odd. He said everyone knows Jesus is not our father's son. What do you think he was talking about?"

She stopped in the doorway, stood for a long moment, then said, "I have no idea. Maybe you should ask Mama."

My head throbbed, and my left eye was swollen shut. I reached up and touched the puffiness around my eye. A sharp pain resonated to my toes. I felt like I had been kicked by a mule, but I knew I had only been hit by one.

I hoped the swelling would go down quickly, but I knew I would probably be a sight for some time. After I ate, I got up and went out into the courtyard. Mama sat at the table near an open fire. The evening sky sparkled as if the heavens were studded with jewels.

"Mama, may I sit with you?"

"Of course." She looked at me with a mixture of love and sympathy. "You probably won't see much out of that eye for a while." She kissed my cheek and added, "Be careful around that well. You don't want to slip again."

"I'll be more careful, Mama. I promise."

I stared at the stars, contemplating how to ask the question Asher had branded in my mind. With every approach I considered, a reason not to use it followed. Maybe the subject should not be addressed.

"Something you want to ask me?" Mama said.

"I don't know how to ask it."

"You have always been able to bring your troubles to me."

"This time is different. I don't want to say something wrong or hurtful. Are there questions that shouldn't be asked?"

"Do you trust me? Are you confident I will always tell you the truth?"

"Yes."

"Then ask. I will never tell you anything but the truth." She put her hand on mine.

"Mama, is Jesus my brother?"

"Yes."

I debated if the next question was necessary. Then, as though someone else spoke, the question came. "Is Papa his father?"

After a long pause, she said, "Yes . . ."

My next breath came with an audible whoosh.

"And no."

Well after everyone else had gone to bed, Mama and I talked, cried, and laughed. If it had been anyone other than Mama, I wouldn't have believed what she said.

∞

The memory of that conversation rested heavy on my heart as a faint rumbling sound came from the direction of the city walls—similar to that of thunder but also like a military caravan departing the city.

I thought I would always view my brother differently after that conversation, and I did for a season. Our days returned to their usual pattern, but I never forgot that evening. And never would.

"Mama, do you remember that evening we talked about Jesus, when you told me about the angelic visit and said he was my brother but my father was not his father?"

"Yes." She squeezed my hand.

"If all you said then is true, I don't understand what happened today. How could his death fit into anything God planned? Why did he die as a thief? He did nothing wrong."

"I desire the answer to that question as much as you do." With a deep sigh, she squeezed my hand. "When God sent his angelic messenger, I could have rejected his words because I didn't understand God's purpose. And I couldn't comprehend why God chose me. Yet in my heart I knew then, as I know now, that neither my will nor my understanding is necessary. Only his and his alone. One day we will know why, but I don't think the explanation will come today."

My confusion about all that I had seen that day, all that had taken place, and all that I had heard was immeasurable. Who was this man I called my brother? Who was his father? Why did his life end so grotesquely?

"I'm not sure, if we had all the answers, it would change anything," I said.

With a platter of fig cakes and a jug of water, Mary and Martha joined us at the table. John awoke, stretched, and sat quietly on the bench at the far wall.

"Come and join us, John." Sensing his hesitancy, I filled a goblet of water and set it next to me. He rose, walked over, and took the seat.

I chose my words carefully and spoke them sincerely, but I could not dispel the humiliation of my mother's care being entrusted to another. Putting my hand on his shoulder, I said, "Thank you, John, for being there for my brother and my family."

Mary rose and winked at me. "I promised I would show you something, James." She disappeared through the courtyard gate.

"I'm so sorry for your loss, Martha," I said. "We received word of your brother's death as we prepared for our trip to Jerusalem. Can I help you and Martha in any way while we are here?"

"God has given us back all we need." Her smile was as enigmatic as Mary's had been when she and I talked of Lazarus's death.

"James," Mary said as she reentered the courtyard, "I said there was something I wanted to show you, but it's really someone."

Lazarus stepped in the entrance, looking better and heathier than I had ever seen him.

"Lazarus," I said, jumping to my feet and running to embrace him. "I don't understand. I heard you were dead."

"I was, James. Not only dead but buried."

With a hand on each shoulder, I pushed him to arm's length. "What?"

"Come, sit." He led me back to the table.

While he bit into a fig cake and took a drink of water, I marveled at his appearance. My father and his father had known each other since they were children. When we traveled near Bethany, we would make a point to spend some time with them.

I had known Lazarus most of my life, and I had never seen him look so well. A pale, frail child, he had always been battling some illness. But the man who sat before me was ruddy and robust.

"You look wonderful, my friend. What did you mean when you said you died and were buried?"

Before responding, Lazarus looked away as though his thoughts drew him back to another time and place. "I had become gravely ill, worse than any other time. My sisters brought physicians, healers, and priests, but my condition did not improve. They sent word to Jesus to come, but before he arrived, I died." Eyes twinkling, he looked at Mary and said, "I don't remember that part."

Martha excused herself, went into the house, and quickly returned holding a neatly folded, tattered, clean burial garment. "We prepared his body," she said, "with all the required ointments and spices and wrapped him in burial cloths."

Tears ran down Mary's cheeks. "Along with our family and many of our friends, we took his body to our family tomb and buried it."

"He had been dead for four days when your brother came," Martha said.

A stillness fell over me as I turned to Lazarus. How could this man have been trapped in a tomb for four days?

"I heard him call my name, as if I were far away and he was beckoning me," Lazarus said. "Suddenly I found myself standing in the daylight, bound in fabric and struggling to get loose."

"It was Jesus," Mary said. "The power of his words— 'Come out!'—gave our brother back to us."

"Since that day, I have felt more alive than ever before," Lazarus said.

I wondered if Lazarus had lost his mind and if it was contagious. The dead brought to life? If that was possible, I was ready to be infected. But how could it be so?

Sensing my doubt, Lazarus smiled. "I know, I know. Hard to believe. But one thing I know is true, and I know you believe it too." With an unmistakable joy in his voice, he added, "Nothing is impossible for God."

"Nothing is impossible for God," I said quietly. Jairus had said the same thing. A little girl and a grown man with three things in common: they were dead, they met my brother, and they lived.

Hours passed. Everyone in the courtyard shared what they had heard and seen, except me. I tried to absorb it all. My imagination filled in the gaps and transformed their words into pictures. Their stories were surreal. My family and our friends could have been speaking of a mythical character, the kind parents create to entertain children. Was that happening here? After witnessing someone you love being nailed to a cross, wouldn't anyone seek the beauty of fantasy to block out the horror of reality?

The following day was the Sabbath. No work could be done, which provided an opportunity to talk with Mama at length. We reminisced about both the good and the bad antics of my siblings and me. Much of what had been perceived as bad had become humorous and harmless recollection. I listened intently to episodes in her life that she had never mentioned. Memories surfaced that Mama had stored away for many years. I treasured every detail of strange encounters, dangers avoided, and divine interventions. She spoke as though each story was connected to the past few days' events, but I struggled to see the correlation. Mama had an understanding that I could not grasp. Perhaps God had given it to her alone.

As the afternoon wore on, others added to the conversation. Mariam spoke of her love and admiration for her eldest brother, and Lazarus shared his appreciation of Jesus's wisdom and compassion for anyone he met. Mary and Martha expressed their affection for him and their devotion, and John told us more stories of the wonders Jesus had performed.

Their stories were uplifting and inspiring but also overwhelming. I could not absorb everything I had heard about my brother over the last two days. How could all this be true of a man who died on a cross as a criminal? There had to be a purpose, an explanation for everything—from the miracles to the murder.

The morning following the Sabbath, I awoke to sounds of activity in the courtyard. I stepped to the door and squinted into a bright, cloudless sky. Mama hurried to me.

"Good morning, James," she said. "I have made you something to eat. Come."

I took a place at the table, and Mama placed some water, figs, and warm bread in front of me. Mariam slid in next to me. "What do you think of what we heard last night about Jesus?" she whispered.

With a mouth full of bread, I shrugged. Too early in the morning to think. Frustrated by my lack of response, Mariam got up and went into the house.

Mama set fruit on the table and took a seat across from me. Her eyes were teary, but in them I saw that familiar determination that rose up when she was about to say or do something she didn't want to. "Mariam and I are going to the tomb to complete the preparations for his burial," she said. "I may need your help."

Jesus's tomb? That was the last place I wanted to go, and burial rites were the last chore I wanted to undertake, but I wouldn't abandon her again. "I'll go and do whatever you need me to do."

"John's going to meet up with some of Jesus's closest friends. They are staying in a home not far from where he is buried. He wants you to go with him and meet all of them. I will not need you until later today."

I was reluctant to leave Mama, but maybe she needed some time to herself, time to mourn privately. "I have met a few of them," I said. "I suppose I could meet a few more."

After clarifying where and when to meet Mama, John and I set out for Jerusalem. Lazarus waited for us at the courtyard gate. "I feel the pain of your loss," he said. "Your brother was much more than a friend. Without him, I don't know what course my life will take."

"Nor do I." I embraced him and turned to leave.

I looked back over my shoulder. Lazarus stepped onto a large stone to elevate himself at the gate and waved goodbye, shouting, "We may not know our course, but we know who does—the One who gives us life."

As John and I walked along, Lazarus's words echoed in my mind: *The one who gives us life.*

Was he referring to God or to my brother? Lazarus may have come out of his tomb, but my brother would not be coming out of his. I believe in the one who gives life, and I know the one who can take it. His name was Pontius Pilate, Rome's governor of Judea.

Jesus called in a loud voice, "Lazarus, come out!" The dead man came out, his hands and feet wrapped with strips of linen, and a cloth around his face. Jesus said to them, "Take off the grave clothes and let him go."

John 11:43–44

CHAPTER TWELVE

Lessons in the Void

The dark sky gave way to the luminous gold of the sun as it rose behind John and me, casting our shadows like tall, thin trees along the path. Who was this man beside me? He was young, yet he had held his ground when everyone else fled. What kind of relationship did he have with my brother? He must have possessed a special place in Jesus's heart. Otherwise, he would not have turned over the care of our mother to this young man.

There must have been a depth in him beyond what I had seen. Martha said Jesus called him and his brother the Sons of Thunder, which indicated an explosive side to this young man. He, along with most of the others who followed my brother, were fishermen. Why fishermen? I did not think there was a single carpenter among his followers.

I stopped and leaned against a tree when we reached the summit. "I need to catch my breath." Bent over, hands on my knees, I wheezed like the collapsing of an empty wineskin. "I prefer going around the mountain rather than over it."

"We can rest a while, but then we must go," he said. "We started later than I wanted to. I had hoped to leave early enough to avoid anyone on the streets."

"Why?"

"The Temple Guard will be looking for all of Jesus's followers, and you can be sure that a good number of Pilate's soldiers will be as well."

"What would Herod's guards or Pilate's centurions want with you?"

"To arrest us."

"What have you done?"

"We have committed our lives to live as God has instructed us and to follow the example he set for us through his son," he said, glancing back to the city. "We must go. Now."

We descended the Mount of Olives and passed through Gethsemane. John pointed to a clearing. "Here is where I last spoke with Jesus. He prayed as we slept." He scanned the area, pain etched on his face. "They arrested him here." Looking heavenward, he cried, "Forgive me, Lord."

I didn't want to add to John's anguish, but I felt compelled to question him. "How did you come to know my brother?"

"My brother James and I were with our father fixing our nets, preparing for a day's catch, when Jesus came and asked what we were doing. James laughed and said, 'We're sheering sheep, can't you tell?'" John said. "Then Jesus reached down, lifted some of the net, and said, 'Come with me and I will show you how to fish for men.'"

I said, "That's it? He just told you to follow him and you did?"

"I knew my life would never be the same, but I felt then, as I do now, that I was born to proclaim his message to all who will hear."

"You told me a lot of interesting stories last night, but you said nothing about a message."

"The wonders I spoke of last night merely confirm the message. It is the message that is all important."

"So . . . what is it?"

John shared my brother's teachings as we walked along the outside of the eastern wall. He spoke of how Jesus brought hope and peace into a world of turmoil and how he promoted a life of service that brought promise and joy.

Although he spoke with passion, his words fell on deaf ears. My hope and joy vanished when my brother was hammered onto a tree. I did not interrupt John's discourse, but I could not understand why he still believed any of it. He had stood at the foot of the cross as any promise of peace was drained from the man who promised it. Yet John held tenaciously to the assurances Jesus had given—maybe because promises were all he had left.

Around the southern end of the Great Wall, we entered the Lower City by way of the Essene Gate. Climbing the rugged slope that divided the Lower from the affluent Upper City, known as Zion, we came to the Essene Quarter. There we entered the spacious home of Mary and her son, Mark, one of Jesus's disciples.

"Wait here," John said.

He investigated the doorways and alleys as well as the faces of those preparing their merchandise for the day's business. "I'll see if they are here. Some do not know you, so I need to tell them about you, then I'll bring you in."

I crossed the street and took a seat on a bench that faced the front door of the home. John ascended an exposed stairway at the side of the building, knocked, and disappeared inside. I wondered if the precautions were necessary, but then I considered what had been done to an innocent man whose only crime was his teachings. I refocused my attention on the street and its inhabitants.

After fifteen or twenty minutes, two young women hurried up the street, approached the front door of the home, and knocked. A woman opened the door and they entered. Within a minute or two, another woman ran to the home, climbed the steps, banged on the door, and was also allowed entrance. Moments later, John and a rugged-looking man burst through the door, descended the steps, and ran north toward the Upper City. Behind them came the woman who had gone into the room at the top of the stairs. She, too, headed north, at a quick pace.

Should I run too? Should I follow them? Maybe the women had warned my brother's followers of approaching soldiers. In that case I should run—in a different direction. But why ? I'd done nothing wrong, except associate with a fisherman who happened to be a close friend of my brother.

"My brother," I said. If merely associating with a friend of my brother could lead to arrest, how much more dangerous to be his brother? I stood, debated which direction to go, and decided to return to Bethany.

"James." A baritone voice from the top of the stairs said. "James, come up."

At the foot of the steps, I hesitated. If others were fleeing from this place, why would I want to be here? I was nothing more than the naive brother of a man wrongly accused and executed. But if Roman soldiers found me inside that house, my presumption of innocence was lost. I needed to go back to Bethany, retrieve Mama and Mariam, do what was necessary for an honorable burial, and return home.

Scanning the street in both directions, every muscle in my body tightened, ready to bolt. "James, please come. We must speak with you."

I looked up at the bearded man at the head of the steps. Another voice rose up from deep within me, echoing off the chambers of my mind: *You have run before. What did that accomplish?*

At the door, I was greeted by a man with scarred, calloused hands and a toothy smile. "Welcome. My name is also James. I'm John's brother. He and Peter just left. They'll be back soon."

"Something wrong?"

"Come in." He opened the door and ushered me into a large, dimly lit room. Patches of morning sunlight fought their way through partially shuttered windows. A musty odor hung in the air—a small price to pay to assure concealment.

Three tables with assorted cushions sat in the room a few paces away from the wall under the windows. The dark outlines of four men reclined at a table at the farthest end of the room. Two more sat across from them in the shadows.

"This is James, the brother of our Lord," James said.

They all rose. Several bowed slightly. A couple of them, whose faces were familiar, came and embraced me.

"James, you may know some here. Simon, Thaddeus, Bartholomew, and another James," he said, pointing to those around the table. "Andrew and Philip," he said, placing his hand on the shoulder of one of the two who had embraced me. "Over there is Matthew." He gestured to a solitary figure staring out a window. The greetings were cordial but cheerless. I could smell the fear in the room, and their somber mood matched mine.

"Let me get you something to drink," Simon said and poured water into a goblet.

"Have you been to the tomb?" Matthew said without turning away from the window.

"I don't even know where it is. I was told that a member of the ruling council allowed his tomb to be used."

"Yes," Simon said. "Joseph of Arimathea, a good man."

Matthew said, "The tomb is on the ridge near Golgotha."

Silence filled the room. The clatter of the merchants outside preparing for the day ahead seemed disrespectful. An unusual stillness settled over me—not tranquil, just quiet. Although there was no movement or sound, the room felt tense. In what felt like minutes, but were probably mere seconds, Andrew broke the silence.

"Your brother's body is missing," he said.

My blood ran cold. "Missing!" I cried out.

"The women went to prepare the body this morning," Andrew said. "Mary returned and said the centurion guard Pilate placed there was gone, and the stone had been rolled away. She said she looked in and saw only the burial garments. Jesus's body was gone."

"Peter and John went to see for themselves," Matthew said from the back of the room. "They should be back soon. We can't go out as a group or we'll be arrested."

"I don't understand. How could he be missing?" I turned to the door. "I have to go. My mother and sister are also going to prepare the body. I can't let them find him missing."

"James, be careful," Thaddeus said. "The high priest has ordered that any follower of Jesus is to be arrested and brought before the council."

"I am not one of his followers," I snapped. "I'm his brother." Opening the door, I turned and looked back. "Why was a guard placed there?"

Andrew said, "To make sure we didn't steal the body."

"Steal the body? Why would you do that?" Anger welled up within me. None of this made sense. I slammed the door behind me.

I walked, then ran in the direction where my brother's life had been snuffed out and his body had been laid to rest. The quickest route was along the outside of the Western Wall, but that would be teeming with pilgrims preparing to return home. I moved as fast as I could, skirting around tables and displays of merchandise in the Essene Quarter, then through the Upper City, past Herod's palace and out through the Gennath Gate. There before me was Golgotha. Below and to the left, inset in the cliff, were individual tombs, some open, some under construction, and some with large round boulders blocking their entrances.

On the dusty cobblestone path, two men headed in my direction. In a voice cracked with emotion, John said, "James, his body has been stolen. We don't know where they have taken him."

"Why would anyone steal a body?"

"We believe it was Joseph Caiaphas, the high priest, who ordered his body taken," said the rugged older man. "The chief priests were afraid we would take it and claim Jesus rose from the dead. They must want to use it as evidence of his death. They may make a public display of his body—most likely in the plaza in front of the steps of the temple."

It took a moment for that horrific thought to settle into my mind. What more could they do? What depravity could their minds conceive to degrade my brother any further?

"Who are you?" I said.

"I am Simon. My brother is Andrew. You can call me Peter—the name Jesus gave me."

"Did you see my mother there? She and my sister were going to prepare his body."

"We saw no one," John said.

"I want to catch them before they get here. I don't want them to find his body missing."

"I understand," John said. "We will return to the house. If we hear anything, we'll send a message to you. Will you be staying in Bethany?"

I nodded. "My mother won't leave until she can give him a proper burial."

"Be cautious, my friend. We do not know who to trust or believe," Peter said. "One of our own betrayed us, and many want to kill those who followed your brother. But wherever we are, you are always welcome to join us."

I stepped aside and let them pass, then sat beside the path watching as they faded from view. Once again my attention was drawn to that detestable mound of earth and the crosses that rose from its crown. I couldn't help but marvel at all that had taken place over the last three days. Even though the sky was clear, I was sure I saw a bolt of lightning streak across the heavens.

Our journey had begun as nothing more than a rescue mission to find a wayward sibling and bring him home. A trial, abuse, and ultimately death followed. With every turn, I met familiar faces, lives that had intersected with mine. In each encounter, a new and distinctive facet of my brother's life was revealed.

Had I ever really known him?

He had been credited with giving sight to the blind, strength and function to crippled limbs, and the breath of life to the dead. They had called him healer, rabbi, and Lord.

Around the evening fire at the home of Martha, John said that Jesus forgave sins and referred to himself as the Son of God. Lazarus, Mary, and Martha believed him to be the promised messiah.

I was raised in Jesus's shadow. I loved, admired, and followed him as my big brother, but could he be the messiah? No. He took being the eldest brother too seriously, and he would say things that made no sense. When he left our home and Mama to embark on an absurd obsession to change the world, it hurt and frustrated the whole family. It broke my heart when, with his last words, he passed Mama's care to another.

Was he the messiah, the Son of God? No. How could that be? A victorious king does not lose the battle before it's fought. If he were the Son of God, how could anyone take his life? That alone proved he was no god.

A desperate need for a savior grows in times of oppression. When ignorance and arrogance nail an innocent man to a tree for voicing an unpopular opinion, people seek a new leader. Of course they would find a messiah to fill the void when hope had died. They had done it before, and many so-called messiahs had appeared. Many more awaited their turn.

But more important concerns were at hand. I had to find Mama and tell her what had happened. Then I needed to seek out Jairus and the centurion and those who could get an audience with members of the council to determine what involvement they had in the disappearance of Jesus's body and where they may have taken it.

If what Peter said was true, then the public humiliation of my brother's body would take place soon, most likely that day.

As I approached Bethany, I saw Mama and Mariam at the well, filling several jugs. How do you tell a mother someone had stolen her dead son's body? I drew near, and she welcomed me with a smile. I put my arms around her and hugged her tight.

"I know that they have taken his body," Mama said. "Some of Mary's friends came shortly after you left and told us."

A mixture of sadness and relief coursed through me. "I will find him."

After an hour of preparation, Lazarus and I set out to return to the city and begin our search. Mama and Mariam would come later and accompany us to the Sanhedrin and to Herod, if necessary. A grieving mother would generate more sympathy than an angry brother. Moreover, some assumed that I and those known as Jesus's disciples would soon occupy a prison cell—or a cross.

At the base of the Mount of Olives, we were confronted by a large caravan of travelers. We greeted them with a wave and moved off the roadway so they and their animals could pass unobstructed. As they walked by, a man at the end of the caravan stepped away and approached us.

"My name is Amir. You are Lazarus?" he said to my companion.

"Yes, I am Lazarus."

"I was present when the master called you forth. I'm honored to speak with you. But you must know your life is in danger. The high priest has placed a bounty on you. You must not go to Jerusalem. It is too dangerous."

I put my hand on Lazarus's shoulder. "He is right. You do not need to place yourself in danger. I can find where they have taken my brother. Return home. I'll send word with what I find."

"He gave me my life," Lazarus said. "He called me from my tomb. How can I refuse to honor him by placing him in his? He must be buried properly."

"You will be present at his interment. For now, return and protect you family."

"Please, sir, you are a symbol of hope," Amir said. "You are the evidence of God's power, promise, and mercy. I beg you, don't go to Jerusalem."

"I will return home, James, if you promise to return by nightfall. It's not safe for you either, especially at night."

"I will see you tonight." We embraced, and the two men blended into the caravan. I set out to find my brother—this time with a far different mission.

I left the customary route and moved west along the base of the Mount of Olives to avoid the congestion of caravan traffic. Traveling north through the Kidron Valley, I reached the winding trail that led to the Golden Gate. When I entered the outer court of Solomon's Portico, a strange hush had fallen over the temple courts. Even though the Passover celebration had ended, the temple grounds were rarely silent, particularly at this time of day.

I exited through the Sheep Gate into the shadows cast by the towers of the Fortress of Antonia. At the wall of the northern tower sat a lone centurion, lance across his lap, helmet on the ground at his side. His head rested on his forearms. Not wanting to startle him, I shuffled my feet noisily as I approached to alert him that I was there, but he did not move.

I stopped in front of him and cleared my throat several times. "Can you help me? I need to speak to someone about my brother."

He raised his head. "What about him?"

"He was crucified and buried two days ago, but someone has taken his body from the tomb."

"You are his brother?" he said, slowly standing and letting his lance fall to the ground.

"Yes. I need to find his body so my mother, sister, and I may bury him according to our tradition."

In a monotone voice, as though his response was rehearsed, he said, "His followers have stolen his body so they can claim he has risen from the dead."

"His followers?"

"Yes," he said. After a long pause he turned away from me, bent down, picked up his lance and helmet, then glanced back at me. His eyes were filled with tears, and his face contorted as though he were in pain.

"Are you sure of that?"

"I was there. At his tomb," he said, pushing his way passed me, disappearing behind the fortress wall.

To solve the mystery of my brother's missing body, I had to start where I had begun that morning—in the room where his followers hid. Moving through the residue of humanity from the Passover festivities, I ascended the steps to the house and banged my fist on the door.

"What do you want?" came a voice from inside.

"I am James, the brother of Jesus."

"Are you alone?"

"Yes."

Someone opened the door and I entered. A pair of troubled eyes scanned me. "Come in."

Inside, I could see only shapes. The shutters were closed, and a blanket of humid heat covered the room. A single candle stood on one of the tables. When my eyes adjusted, I counted far more bodies than had been present on my first visit.

I did not waste time on greetings or introductions. "A centurion told me that some of you took my brother's body so you can say he has risen from the dead. Is this true?" I looked around the room. Every eye focused on me. Did they consider me a threat—or should I feel threatened?

Stepping out of the shadows, Peter said, "No, that is not true. We are as saddened and sickened as you. We loved him and he loved us. We would not do anything to defame his name or cause anyone to question what he has taught or done."

"But we have gotten word that some claim to have seen him." Another voice spoke from the dark.

"What?

"Pay no mind to that," Peter said. "Some of the women said they saw someone they believe was Jesus, but they also said they saw angels."

"I don't want Mama to hear those stories. It is difficult enough for her to deal with the death of her son, but to put some false hope in her heart is cruel."

"Agreed," Peter said.

"Where can I go? Who do I seek out that I may know where they have taken his body? My mother and sister will enter the city soon seeking an audience with the Council, maybe even with Pilate. I want to find Jesus's body before any of that is necessary."

John stepped to my side and placed his arm around my shoulder. "We understand, but we don't know any more than you do. Peter and I went to the tomb when we heard it was empty but found nothing. Have you been there?"

I shook my head.

"Go there. You may find someone who has the answers you seek," John said.

"As good a place as any to start," I said. "What do you plan to do?"

"We will remain here and pray. God gave us direction when we needed it most, and we are confident he will do so now," Peter said. "You will be in our prayers as well."

After several introductions and a number of sympathetic gestures, I set my course for the tomb. Traversing through the Upper City and then the Gennath Gate, I rounded the corner of the northwest wall and there before me was the garden where the tomb was located.

In the distance, a figure walked toward me. Within several minutes, I realized the person was a woman moving rather quickly. Soon the form became familiar. I would recognize that gait anywhere. Mariam. What was she doing here, and where was Mama?

"James!" she shouted. "James!"

She was breathless when she drew near, her face radiant. "We found him."

"Where is his body?" I said, assuming Mama would be there.

"Oh, it's not his body. It's him."

"What do you mean 'it's him'?"

"Come," she said, pulling my arm as we walked. "Hurry! Mama is waiting for us."

I pulled back and slowed my pace. "Mariam slow down," I said, taking her arm and causing her to stop. "Where is Mama, and what are you talking about?"

"When we arrived at the tomb this morning, the stone had been moved, so I went in while Mama sat outside. I was there but a few seconds because it was empty. When I came out, Mama was standing and looking toward the city. She told me Jesus came and talked with her. He said he would return to see her again. He's alive, James!" She began to squeal excitedly. "He's alive! Isn't that wonderful?"

"Did you see him?

"No," she said. "Mama told me to find you. She didn't want to leave the tomb."

"You were inside the tomb for a few seconds, and when you came out, he wasn't there?"

"That's right," she said. "But Mama said—"

"I don't think you should have left her alone."

When we arrived, Mama sat on a large, flat stone. The chisel marks on its side indicated it was the tomb's entrance cover. Her smile spoke of peace and contentment. I had seen that tenderness in times of effervescent joy and deep sorrow. It always encouraged me.

"Mama, are you all right?"

"Yes. Did Mariam tell you?"

"She told me," I said, hesitant to discuss the apparition of my brother there at his tomb. "I want you to go back to Bethany. Please. I have a few things to do in the city, but I will be there before sunset. We can talk then."

"James, he is alive. Your brother is alive."

"I know, I know," I said to appease her. "I want you and Mariam to go with one of the caravans that will travel east past Bethany so you will be safe." I knew they could make the journey alone; after all, they had gotten here safely, but that was before she found the tomb empty.

Mama's grief was immeasurable. She had witnessed her son's execution and, at his tomb, found someone had stolen his body. Was it any wonder she would hallucinate, desperate for some measure of hope? I was concerned for her to return with only Mariam at her side. I would have gone with them, but I had to find Jesus's body. He should have been buried within eight hours after he was taken from the cross, and three days had passed.

"I will help you find an appropriate family procession to join. Please, Mama. We can talk about this later."

"James, my son, this cannot be put aside for later. Your brother has risen from the dead. Do you understand that?" Her tone was both excited and desperate.

"Mama, stop. Stop," I said, concern heavy in my voice. "I understand what you say you saw, but I am responsible for you, and I want you to go back to Mary and Martha's. I will follow shortly."

Mama reached up, took a gentle hold of my ear, pulled me down to her, and kissed my cheek. "James, I understand your concern, and I will do as you ask. You do not need to search for him. He will find you."

"I won't let her out of my sight," Mariam said.

I accompanied them around the northern wall to the base of Gethsemane. Taking note of the provisions the various travelers packed, I surveyed the assembled families as they prepared for their journey home. The larger the provision, the further they would be traveling. I felt more comfortable with those who lived reasonably close. They were more like neighbors than sojourners. I found a family of ten from Khirbet Qumran and asked if my mother and sister could accompany them to Bethany. They agreed, and after I introduced them, all the ladies joined in casual conversation.

Would Mama speak of the encounter with her dead son? After I hugged Mariam, I embraced Mama and whispered, "Please don't tell anyone else what you saw. I promise I will find him."

I watched the small caravan grow faint in the distance and tried to process Mama's words. I walked to the entrance of the garden of Gethsemane and gazed at the eerie shadows cast by the swaying trees. In the distance, thunder rumbled across the horizon. "Leftovers from the afternoon storm, no doubt," I said.

An air of peaceful calm settled around me. The distant, muffled noise that originated from the Great City had gone silent. Even the wind had stopped. The leaves and the branches were no longer moving, and the birds had ceased their incessant chatter.

"James."

My name seemed to hang in the air like a feather floating to the ground. The voice that uttered my name was one I knew well.

"James."

My heart began to hammer in my chest, and I could barely breathe. My legs trembled, and I almost lost my balance. I didn't want to turn around. I was terrified of what I might see. I closed my eyes and felt my face flush. I began to sweat, and butterflies took wing in my stomach. I thought I was going to be sick.

"James."

It couldn't be him; no one could survive what he went through. Another wave of fear washed over me, and I was suddenly gripped by a desperate urge to run, but I couldn't move.

Once again, that familiar voice spoke my name, gently, "James."

I tried to control my breathing and calm my heart as I slowly turned. I kept my eyes shut, dreading what I was about to see.

"Don't be afraid, little brother," he said.

I opened my eyes, and there before me stood my brother. His smile was warm and inviting. There was hope in his eyes, and I could feel his love for me. My fear just went away, and in its place was an overwhelming sense of peace and joy.

His hair was not matted with blood but washed, and there was no remnant of the thorns that had pierced his head. The blackened bruises and swelling around his eyes and face were gone. There were no open wounds caused by the beatings he received, but his hands, though cleansed, had the deep, exposed gashes made by Roman spikes.

"I . . . I saw you die."

"Yes, you did."

"I saw them kill you."

"Yes, they did."

Tears blurred my vision as I threw my arms around him and kissed his neck.

Pushing me to arm's length, he said, "There is much more to be done, little brother. I have come to you so that you might believe. You know me better than most, but do not let that stand in the way of listening to your heart."

Together we walked in silence through a small grove of olive trees. A myriad of questions, issues, and uncertainties swirled in my head. I slowed my pace just enough to study his profile. His face was not torn or bruised as it had been on the cross; neither were his robes matted in dried blood. On the contrary, he was clothed in the whitest robe I had ever seen. I glanced down and saw the open wounds in his feet where large nails had been driven through them, yet his walk was sure and firm, without any indication of pain or discomfort.

We sat in the shade of a large olive tree that overlooked the city wall. The temple dome glistened in the sun. I do not know when it happened, but I was no longer plagued by unanswered questions. A deep, reverent peace had settled over me as a cool breeze brought the scent of roses.

"Tell me, little brother. What have you learned in your journey between the lightning and the thunder?"

The question may have confused some people, but I knew exactly what he meant. I had spent the last three days in that void between the lightning and the thunder, encountering familiar faces and reflecting on days long past. I had heard tales only God could orchestrate and listened to testimonies of miraculous interventions in broken lives. Legs that never walked could now dance with joy. Hands that had never held loved ones now embraced them. Eyes that had never seen now watched the morning sunrise. Lips that had never spoken now sang God's praises. Jesus's followers spoke of hearts darkened in despair, crushed by rejection and loss, but now filled with hope and thanksgiving. Precious lives taken far too early by death's final blow and locked away in the catacombs for eternity had risen to new life as evidence of God's power and mercy.

"What have I learned between the lightning and the thunder? I have learned of a man I did not know, though we grew up in the same home. I have learned of a man accused of being a drunkard and a threat, yet his love and compassion brought healing to those his accusers would not touch. This man was beaten and abused, but he healed those who were battered by life. I have learned of a man who was put to death on a cross, yet he gave life back to the dead. A man whose heart was pierced by the pain of others before it was pierced by a Roman lance. I saw that man die, yet now he sits beside me."

"I love you, brother," I said.

I sank to my knees, placing my hands on the ground at his feet and bowing my head in both honor and shame. I tried to maintain some measure of composure, but I couldn't. I wept. I couldn't stop. I didn't want to.

The release was wonderful. I had never felt that way.

I was free.

After several minutes, the pounding of my heart became a steady beat, my breathing returned to normal, and the butterflies departed. Although the tears continued to flow, and I didn't want to leave his side, I stood with the feeling that there was more to be done.

Jesus stood and looked me in the eye. "I have watched you these last several days, your conflicts and struggles. You let nothing or no one stand in the way of completing the task that lay before you. With that same resolve and tenacity, you must follow me."

I saw no judgment or condemnation in his eyes. Just acceptance and empathy. And love. He was not asking for anything; he was giving everything. He wasn't seeking something from me; he was seeking me.

"James, your time has come." He placed the palm of his hand on my chest. "My Father has given you life and the free will to live it as you choose. You have been guided to see and hear from those whom you know and who know me. Now you must make a choice. I will always love you, James. You are my brother. But now you must choose. Who are you? Who do you say that I am?"

I looked at the hand that rested upon my chest and at the open wound made by a Roman nail. My lungs heaved for air when I tried to speak.

What had I learned between the lightning and the thunder? What choice had I made? As I lifted my face to meet his gaze, the words flowed freely with no reserve.

"I am James, a servant of God and my Lord, Jesus, who is the Christ."

James, a servant of God and of the Lord Jesus Christ,
To the twelve tribes scattered among the nations:
Greetings.
James 1:1

ACKNOWLEDGMENTS

Now I have the opportunity to acknowledge and thank those who have been instrumental in bringing this literary endeavor into existence. There are far too many to list, but you know who you are and that I treasure our friendship and your support. Here are a few of those who pushed, prodded, edited, and coached me along the way:

Donna Stephens, thank you for your prayers and encouragement not to let it go to seed.

Reese Johansen, thank you for not letting up. Your persistence pushed me to the goal.

Laurie Hughes, thank you for igniting the flame to write—a flame that had long gone out.

Larry J. Leech II, thank you for your hours of coaching, counsel, and friendship.

Roberta Randall, thank you for believing in me, and not allowing me to think it couldn't be done.

Iron Stream Media and Brookstone Creative Group, thank you for your excellent coaching staff.